AMBER
AND THE
HIDDEN CITY

....

BY
MILTON J. DAVIS

Milton J. D— 11/9/2020

YOUNG LIONS PRESS

Young Lions Press, LLC
Fayetteville, Georgia

MVmedia, LLC
PO Box 1465
Fayetteville, GA 30214
www.mvmediaalt.com

Publisher's Note: This is a work of fiction. Names, characters, places, and incidents are a product of the author's imagination. Locales and public names are sometimes used for atmospheric purposes. Any resemblance to actual people, living or dead, or to businesses, companies, events, institutions, or locales is completely coincidental.

Book Layout ©2017BookDesignTemplates.com

Ordering Information:
Quantity sales. Special discounts are available on quantity purchases by corporations, associations, and others. For details, contact the "Special Sales Department" at the address above.

Amber and the Hidden City/Milton J. Davis. –2nd ed.
ISBN 978-0980084276

Contents

To My Ladies, Vickie and Alana

CHAPTER ONE

One more goal, that's all they needed. Amber Robinson bounced on the balls of her feet while the referee placed the ball on center field. Her brown face glistened with sweat as she glanced at her companion, forward and best friend, Jasmine Santos. She grinned, and Jasmine threw up a peace sign. This was perfect, Amber thought. There were only her teammates and the game, a challenge she was more than up to. On the field she didn't have to be pretty or charming or graceful. She didn't have to care how her hair looked, if her nails were the right color or if she wore the right perfume. All she had to do was win. The other pressures of her life faded as soon as the referee blew the whistle to start the game. Her hand went absently to Grandma's necklace, the namesake jewels cool against her slender neck, their touch calming her mind. She was ready.

"Okay ladies!" Coach Penny shouted. "Get focused! Let's take this home!"

For the first time since the girls' soccer program began the Wayne Middle School Silverbacks were competing for the Preston County Middle School championship. Cars, minivans and trucks packed the parking lot of Silverback Stadium, an anomaly for a girls' middle school soccer game. The cloudless sky and crisp air set the stage for what the Silverbacks hoped would be their victory to claim. Their sudden success was mainly due to Amber and Jasmine. Jasmine was a soccer prodigy, the daughter of two soccer standouts, her Brazilian father and Jamaican mother and a recent transfer.

Amber, while not as good as Jasmine, was a skilled passer and a perfect judge of opposing players. She had an instinct, Coach Penny said, to read a player's mind. The team depended on her to size up their adversaries and give advice on strategy. Together they were unstoppable.

The referee blew the whistle to begin the second half. Jasmine and the opposing forwards rushed the ball. Amber nodded at Jasmine as she trotted behind them. Jasmine let the Georgetown Jaguar forward take the ball. Amber waited until the Jaguar forward attempted to pass the ball across the field then sprinted to intercepted it. She kicked it forward in a looping arc, the ball falling right before Jasmine. Her friend quickly displayed the dribbling skills she was known and feared for, dancing her way through the Jaguars. Amber ran as fast as she could, knowing Jasmine's good fortune wouldn't last. She watched Jasmine jump, avoiding a vicious sliding tackle then with the flip of her right foot sent the ball streaking toward Amber. The ball was high as it was meant to be. Amber took a deep breath then executed a perfect bicycle kick, sending the ball back to Jasmine as the crowd gasped and roared. The goalie never stood a chance. Jasmine, her back turned to the goal, trapped the ball on her left foot then spun about. The ball left her foot like a pitcher's fastball, speeding by the diving goalie then into the net. The Silverback fans went wild.

The rest of the match was a lesson in perfection. The Silverback defense turned back a couple of spirited attacks by the opposing team and Amber and Jasmine scored three more goals. Extra time was added because of penalties but the game was all but over. When the time ran out the score read 4 – 2, the Silverbacks fans leaping to their feet cheering and waving their silver and black pom-poms. The team rushed the field, for once ignoring Coach Penny's advice of cool decorum after a victory. They'd won the championship; there was no reason for holding back.

Jasmine ran at Amber then leaped into her arms. She shook her fist in the air as Amber struggled to hold her up.

"You know you ain't no petite girl," Amber shouted.

She let go and Jasmine dropped to her feet.

"I know you didn't just insult me," Jasmine said in mock anger.

"If I didn't, who would?"

Jasmine was about to fire back when their teammates overwhelmed them. The two of them were lifted in the air as the team chanted.

"Silverbacks, we bad! Who bad? We bad!"

The team put them down and they broke into a line dance they'd practiced in secret for weeks. Coach Penny walked up to them shaking her head while trying to suppress a grin.

"Okay ladies, that's enough. You're on the verge of unsportsmanlike conduct. Now line up so we can shake hands with our worthy opponents."

They did as they were told. Amber was the first in line. Her response to the opposing team members varied based on her feelings; some a simple high five, others a handshake, and a few a heartfelt hug. Some people just needed to be hugged.

The last person in line was the opposing team's coach. The red faced round man extended his hand.

"Good game, 42," he said. "You're a fine player. Coach Peterson at Julian High will be happy to have you."

The coach's words put a damper on her joy. She wouldn't attend Julian High. Her parents had other plans.

She blocked the bad feelings from her mind, following Coach Penny and the team to the podium.

"Amby! Amby!"

Amber rolled her eyes. "Oh God!"

Jasmine appeared beside her then gave her a gentle jab with her elbow.

"Mommy's calling you," she chided.

Amber looked to the visitor's sideline and spotted Mama. She was fashionably dressed as always, jumping up and down waving silver and black pompoms, reliving her days as a cheerleader. Standing beside her, to Amber's surprise, was her Daddy. He missed most of her games because of work travel, but he'd made it for the championship game as he promised. He towered over Mama, wearing dress shirt and slacks, his tie loosened. He waved the pompom that Mama forced in his hand. He'd obviously come straight from the airport, but that didn't matter. He was here. He kept his promise. She ran to them, jumping into her father's open arms.

"You made it!" she squealed.

"Of course I did. I couldn't miss the best player in the best game."

He spun her around then placed her on her feet.

Mama wrapped her in a tight hug then swayed with her from side to side.

"Congratulations, baby!" she squealed. "You were so great out there!"

"Thank you, Mama," she said, squeezing Mama tight.

"Congratulations, baby girl," Daddy said. He wrapped her and Mama in his thick arms.

"Did you see that bicycle kick?" Amber asked.

"Yes, we did," Daddy said with a grin on his face.

"It was nice, wasn't it?"

"That's your child," Mama said. "So modest."

"No reason to be modest when you're good," Daddy replied. "It was excellent, baby."

They gathered around the podium as Coach Penny received the trophy. She gave a short speech then raised the trophy high. Amber, her teammates and the Silverback fans gave a rousing cheer and the hugs began again.

The Silverbacks paraded to their cars. The coach led the procession to Partner Pies Pizza, the perfect place for a championship celebration. The procession pulled into the driveway then everyone piled out of their cars then lined up to enter the restaurant. As they surrounded their reserved tables Amber's Daddy waved his arms for attention.

"Pizza is on me!" Daddy shouted. A cheer rose over the usual cacophony of the popular pizzeria as the girls and their families took their reserve tables. Jasmine and Amber sat side by side, their parents flanking them. Amber was about to sip her sweet tea when Jasmine elbowed her.

"Girl! You almost made me spill my drink!"

Jasmine nodded her head. "Check it out. Somebody's giving you the serious stink eye."

Amber looked in the direction of Jasmine's nod. Apparently, a few of Georgetown Middle School players chose Partners Pizza Pie for their defeat consolation meal. The girl giving Amber the stink eye was the defensive forward playing opposite her, the one she faked out with the spectacular bicycle kick. Amber looked directly at her then raised her glass.

"Look at you trying to start something," Jasmine whispered.

"I'm just being gracious," Amber replied.

The pizzas arrived moments later. Amber shared a super supreme with Jasmine while the house band played an anemic version of a recent dub step song. Amber wiped her mouth after her fifth slice.

"Potty break!" she shouted.

Mama glared at her.

"Sorry. Excuse me," she said properly.

Amber made her way to the narrow hallway where the restrooms were located. She was about to enter the women's bathroom when the unfriendly faces of the Georgetown Middle School Panthers players appeared. Amber tried to ignore them, but the forward she embarrassed blocked her way. The girl was at least a foot taller than Amber with straw blond hair and a boyish freckled face.

"Excuse me," she said, then entered the restroom.

The Georgetown girls followed her into the restroom. The forward jumped between her and the stall.

"Okay 42, you trying to be all that on the field. What you got now?"

Amber closed her eyes then took a deep breath.

"Sorry, Grandma," she whispered.

The forward grabbed for her. Amber stepped back then kicked the forward's feet from under her then grabbed the second girl by the wrist, forcing her down on top of the other girl. The goalie charged at Amber, her hand outstretched.

"Stay over there!" Amber warned. She stuck out her hand; her necklace warmed around her neck then the goalie stopped, lifted off her feet then slammed into the bathroom door. The girl looked at Amber terrified. Amber looked at her hand the same way.

She was still staring at her hand when the other girls scrambled off the floor, gathered the goalie then ran. Amber went into the stall, trembling as she sat. Before Grandma taught her wrestling she made her promised never to use it unless she was in serious trouble. She had even put up with some bullying just to keep Grandma's promise. But this other thing? She had no idea where that came from.

"Okay Amber, what was that all about?" she whispered. She waited in the stall, listening as people came in and out before finally opening the stall door. To her relief the bathroom was empty. She hurried out then back to the table.

"What took you so long?" Jasmine asked.

Amber shrugged then focused on eating her pizza. The band went into a halfway decent rendition of 'Ain't No Stopping Us Now' and Amber looked up to see Coach Penny holding the microphone.

"Okay Silverbacks, time to show your old coach that dance you were doing!"

The tables emptied immediately. Mama grabbed Amber's hand.

"Come on, baby. Let's show these folks how to move."

She grabbed Daddy's hand, too. Daddy smiled then stood.

"Let's do it," he said.

Amber couldn't keep feeling bad now. She led her parents to the floor then joined in with her teammates, the grownups laughing as they tried to learn the steps and keep pace. Amber scanned the dancers and smiled even though sadness rested on her chest. She was going to miss them so much. But another thought came to her as well. She had to talk to Grandma. Soon.

CHAPTER TWO

Marai, Jewel of the Bright Country, mourned with the morose cadence of the royal djembes. The gleaming towers piercing the expansive canopy grieved as well, their peaks shrouded in black cloaks of cotton cloth. From the edge of the barrier walls to the center of the palace peaks, the city witnessed an event that had not occurred in a thousand years; the Sana, ruler of The Good People, was dying.

The elders of the twelve districts waited the customary twelve days before approaching the palace walls, each an entourage of twelve. They wore the mourning shroud; a simple white cloak trimmed in the color of their district and their clan. Their mourning masks were carved by the Daal, the embellished expressions of grief hiding the wearers' true feelings. It was well known that even though the Sana had been a wise and generous man throughout his rule, there were those that despised him. The day of his death would be a celebration to them, a day that would embark the Good People on a new future. Most of all, those who hated the Sana wished his death for one reason only. A new Sana would mean a new beginning. A new Sana would mean the end of Marai's exile from the world.

Jele Jakada, royal medicine priest of Marai, looked down from his tower onto the noble congregation at the gates. Someone among them would be the next Sana, the man or woman who would either keep the traditions of the city or expose it to the world beyond the walls. He trudged to his stool and sat, cradling his old face in his wrinkled hands.

"I should have called you back, Alake," he whispered. "I'm a stubborn old man who may have doomed us all."

A gentle rapping on his door broke his mood.

"Who is it?" he shouted.

"A servant from the Margara," the voice replied. "She wishes to see you immediately."

Jakada sighed. "So, it begins." He stood, straightening out his robes and arranging his talisman necklaces.

"Tell the Margara I will be along momentarily. I have a few things to attend to."

"Yes, Jele."

Jakada entered a second room, a space crowded with the tools of his craft. At the back of the room stood an object covered by a splendid woven shroud embroidered with symbols and figures telling the story of Marai's history. He took a deep breath and pulled the shroud aside, revealing a large mirror trimmed with ebony wood. Jakada studied his reflection for a moment then closed his eyes as he waved his hands across the smooth surface.

"Come home, my daughter," he chanted. "Your time has come."

* * *

Corliss Johnson awoke that Saturday morning with a head full of memories. She shuffled through her cottage, opening her blinds to the rising sun then proceeded to her bathroom, performing her morning ritual that had shortened over the years. As a young girl she obsessed over her looks; as a wife her attentions ebbed and flowed with the attentions of her husband; but as an old widow she no longer cared what others said about her appearance. She was at the age where the only opinion that mattered was her own.

On that particular day other memories intruded, images of a life she fled long ago. As she dressed in a pair of worn jeans and an Atlanta Braves t-shirt she wondered why she would have those thoughts, memories she assumed she'd hidden away long ago. She was neither afraid nor remorseful, for she had come to terms with her decision. The only nagging resentment was that she had broken with her father. She never tried to contact him, nor he her. In the beginning the pain of his silence cut deep. She couldn't understand how he would let her go without demanding her return. He had always let her have her way, but she thought this one act would rouse him to give her the attention she felt she deserved. Instead there was silence. That was long ago; marriage and children had dulled that pain and healed the wound.

Bean met her at the door as she emerged into the Hilton Head Island summer morning. The cocker spaniel climbed her leg, anxious for his head rub which she obliged. She adopted the tan bundle of spirit from the local pound the day after Travis died, indulging herself with the only pleasure he had never provided her.

"Such a good boy," she said.

"Hello Miss Johnson."

Corliss looked into the eyes of Javan, one of the local concierges of the Sunrise Resort. She liked Javan; he reminded her of home. His deep brown skin, tightly curled hair and prominent lips displayed his Mandingo roots, though if asked Javan would have no idea of what she spoke. He was like all the others, blind to his heritage and stumbling about the land in search of foundation. But he was a pleasant, polite boy, at least to her, and that mattered most.

"Good morning, Javan. Are you my ride?"

Javan tipped his baseball cap. "Yes ma'am. Hey Bean!"

Bean ran to the golf cart and leapt in the back seat. Corliss took her time; Javan helped her inside.

They drove through the resort, waving at the residents as they made their way to the nature trail leading to the Sunrise Beach. Corliss made it a point to know everyone in the resort. She greeted the newcomers with her famous chocolate chip cookies and was one of the main cooks for the resort Thanksgiving dinner. She took the time to build a family around her despite the fact that her son and daughters had moved away long ago. She knew how important family was; to her, family was the only reason to live.

Bean jumped from the cart before it came to a complete stop, charging down the sandy palmetto lined path leading to the beach. The smell of the sea tantalized her senses. After twenty years living along the shore the sea kept its hypnotic effect on her. Javan helped her out of the cart.

"How long you going to be?" he asked.

"Don't worry about me," she answered. "Me and Bean will walk back."

"Okay, Miss Corliss. Have a great day!" Javan waved then sped away.

"Are you sure?"

"I'm sure. Go on now, and thank you for the ride."

Javan tipped his hat, climbed back into the golf cart then sped away.

As Corliss strolled down the path, the nearness of the rolling waves soothed the aches and pains that had become common with advancing age, the salty air a salve to her body. Her pace increased as she neared the waves; by the time she emerged from the sea oat covered dunes she was trotting behind Bean, a wide smile on her face.

"Come home, my daughter. Your time has come."

The words struck her like a fist and she fell onto her knees. She shook her head, attempting to fling away what was obviously an old memory that had escaped its mental confinement.

"This is no memory," the voice announced. *"This is your baba, Alake. It is time for you to come home."*

Corliss jerked about as she searched for her father. There was no mistaking the source for he used her oriki name, a name no one in this world or her old world would have knowledge of. Either it was her father or she was finally going mad.

"You are as sane as the day you left me," he said.

19

Bean returned to her, barking for her to play. She ignored him, looking into the horizon towards her former home.

"Baba, why are you calling for me?"

"You are needed, my child. The Sana is dying."

The mention of the ruler of Marai shattered the mental wall erected long ago. She was awash in her past life, flooded by feelings of loneliness and confinement. She had been a privileged young girl shackled by tradition and duty, her only way out to escape into a world forbidden to her.

Corliss straightened, a stern look coming to her gentle face. "The Sana's fate is no longer my concern," she said. "I am of this world now."

"True, you cannot save the Sana. He is old and weak and the ancestors no longer favor him. But a new Sana must be selected. It is your duty to choose."

"Can you see me, baba?" she asked.

There was a moment of silence before he answered. *"Yes, Alake, I can see you. I stand before the mirror."*

"Then you know I am no longer a girl. I am older than you. I have neither the strength nor the nyama to choose a new Sana."

"The bloodline belongs to you."

Guilt rose in her breast and she pushed it back. "Choose someone else."

"There is no one else."

They were silent for a time, Corliss absently rubbing Bean's head.

"Do you have a daughter?"

"My children know nothing of my past."

"You told them nothing?" Her father's tone was judgmental.

"There was no need for them to know."

"Listen to me, Alake. It is very important that you or a female of your blood return to Marai to select the new Sana. If a Seer does not select him, the council will, and they will choose Bagule."

Terror appeared in her mind, images planted by her father. She saw cities burning and people dying, slain by a Maraibu army led by Bagule.

"These people are not like us," she protested. "They have wonderful machines and lethal weapons. They would crush Bagule."

"Don't be fooled by items built by the hands of men. Weapons of spirit crush a man's soul. Without the spirit to fight a weapon is useless. When I chose to seal Marai from the world it was not to protect us from others. It was to protect the others from us."

The weight of fear and guilt worried Corliss. She remembered all the wondrous things she saw her father perform and she imagined that same power in the hands of someone as vile as Bagule. If he was chosen Sana, her father would have to obey him.

"My daughters know nothing of my past," she repeated. "They would not believe anything I tell them at this point."

"You must convince them."

"I cannot," Corliss confessed. "But my granddaughter is a different matter altogether."

"Is she of age?"

Corliss smiled when she imagined Crystal's daughter. "She would be a woman in our world. Here she is still a child."

"Why do you feel she will believe you?"

"Because I told her of Marai as a child," Corliss answered. "My past was her bedtime stories. Besides, she wears the necklace."

She imagined the surprise on her father's face before he spoke.

"You gave her the Key?"

"I had no intentions of returning."

"You must send her immediately."

"It will take time, baba."

"We have no time."

"Then you must make time," Corliss snapped. "This is no small thing I must do."

"I will help you."

21

Corliss had no idea how he could but she said nothing. "I will send for her. She will be available soon and her parents will be thankful for the respite. How will I contact you?"

"I will be watching, Alake."

Corliss decided to ask the question that haunted her ever since she left her home. "Why didn't you try to stop me from leaving, baba?"

"You were meant to go. In truth, I could not keep you safe in Marai. Bagule has planned his ascension for some time. You would have been the first he would have sought to eliminate. I could not hide you in Marai, but I could hide you in the world."

Corliss was shocked. "You let me go?"

"Yes."

Corliss eyes glistened. "I will send my granddaughter. This I promise you."

"What is your granddaughter's name?" he asked as his voice faded.

"Amber."

CHAPTER THREE

Summer was only a week old but Amber thought it was passing too fast. She lay in her bed in a t-shirt and gym shorts listening to her iPhone and brooding. Private school wasn't her idea. Julian High School was a great school, one of the best in the Metro Area. She researched it for days then presented her argument to her parents, once again trying to secure a happy and rewarding future outside the confines of private school. She got the same response.

"We know Julian High is a great school," Mama would say. "That's the reason we moved here."

"But Clifton Academy offers so much more," Daddy would finish. "You'll have the chance to attend an Ivy League prep school and their soccer program is first rate. It's a win-win, baby girl."

"Your father and I have worked hard for this opportunity," Mama would finish. "We only want the best for you."

What was best for her was Julian High with her friends.

The bedroom door opened and Mama entered with a frown on her face. Amber took off her earphones.

"The world would come to an end and you wouldn't know until you saw wings on your back."

"You're assuming I'd be in Heaven," Amber replied with a wink.

"You got that smart attitude from your Daddy. It's going to get you time out just like him. Jasmine's here."

Amber tumbled off the bed, and then followed Mama downstairs into the kitchen. Jasmine sat at the kitchen table with a Julian High Tigers t-shirt on, a big grin on her face.

"You're so mean!" Amber exclaimed. "You're not my friend anymore. I hate you."

Mama laughed. "Y'all take that upstairs."

Amber turned up her nose as she walked back upstairs. Jasmine followed.

"And Jasmine, talk your friend into fixing her hair. She looks a mess."

"I agree, Mrs. Greene. She does look a mess. I'll do my best."

Amber snarled at Jasmine then trotted upstairs. She flopped onto her bed; Jasmine grabbed the desk chair then rolled it beside the bed.

"I wish I'd seen you," Amber said. "I wouldn't have let you in."

"Even for this?" Jasmine held up another Julian High t-shirt.

Amber squealed then snatched the t-shirt out of Jasmine's fingers. She took off her t-shirt and donned Jasmine's gift.

"Now that's what's up!" she said.

She plugged her iPhone into the speaker system on her dresser, filling the room with smooth soul sounds.

"You want to go swimming?" Jasmine asked.

"No." Amber fell back onto her bed.

"Come on, girl. Stop sulking. It is what it is. We might as well enjoy the summer. Donny's going to be there."

"So?"

"Donny is fine. We can look at him."

"You're so boy crazy. Donny is a jerk."

"That's true, but he's still fine. We don't have to talk to him."

Her phone buzzed on her desk. Amber had no idea who would call her this time of day except Jasmine and she was already in her room. She trudged to the desk and looked at the number.

"Grandma!" she exclaimed. She snatched up the phone then answered. "Hey Grandma!"

"Hey Amber. How's my favorite grandchild doing?"

"I'm okay," she answered.

"You still sulking about private school?"

Amber frowned. "Yeah, but I'll be okay."

"Well, I have a remedy for that. How about you come down and spend a few weeks with me? We'll swim, shop and do a little traveling nearby."

Amber bounced around the room.

"What?" Jasmine asked. "What?"

"Yes!" Amber said. "No, wait a minute. We're supposed to go visit Daddy's family this summer."

"The whole summer?" Grandma asked.

"Yes, ma'am."

"Let me talk to your Mama."

Amber covered the phone. "I'll be right back."

She hurried downstairs to the kitchen. Mama was making lunch, slicing apples and arranging them on a plate.

"Mama, it's Grandma. She wants me to visit."

Mama frowned. "She knows we're going to Martha's Vineyard this summer. Give me the phone."

Amber handed the phone to Mama.

"Hey Mama...Amber just told me. You know we're going to visit Sam's folks...yes, in July, but Amber needs to spend some time at home..."

Amber shook her head vigorously. "I want to go to see Grandma!" she whispered.

Mama held up her hand and Amber fell silent.

"Mama...don't do that Mama, that's not fair...I know I said I was coming...okay Mama, I'll talk to Sam. Love you, too Mama. Bye."

Mama handed her phone back then huffed.

"That woman makes me so mad sometimes," Mama said. She looked at Amber. "You didn't hear that."

Amber didn't care. "Can I go?"

"You sure you don't want to stay here until we go visit?"

"I want to go see Grandma," she said. "I need to relax before we go up north. You know how Daddy's folks are."

Mama looked disappointed. "What do you have against your father's family?"

"Nothing, except they think they're better that everyone else because they happen to trace their family back to some Pullman porter who had a good job back then and for some odd reason that's supposed to give them some kind of status."

"Okay, so they're stuck up," Mama replied. "They're good people and they're crazy about you."

Amber decided to play her trump card. She gazed into her mother's eyes, pouting her lips as she swayed from side to side.

"Can I go to Grandma's? Please?"

"I'll talk to your Daddy tonight. Now go back upstairs. Jasmine came to see you."

Daddy wasn't happy but he relented, succumbing to Amber's sad, watery eyes. Grandma sent her first-class airline tickets the following week, sending Amber into a joy dance. She'd never flown first class before, so she was looking forward to an additional new experience. She was set to leave a week after Grandma's call, her suitcases packed to capacity. The plan was that she would spend two weeks with Grandma then fly to Martha's Vineyard. Grandma wasn't happy about it, but Daddy could be pushed only so much.

Jasmine came to see her the night before she left for Grandma's. They sat on her bed, sharing Jasmine's iPhone through a pair of earphones. For a while smooth neo soul sounds flowed into their ears as they bobbed from side to side. The video games and books that normally cluttered her dresser top were packed away, the piles of clothes usually filling her chairs packed into her royal blue suitcases standing at the foot of her bed. Jasmine took off her earphones and waved for Amber to do the same.

"I wish you were staying home," she said. "I'm going to miss you."

"I wish I was staying, too. But I'd rather go to Grandma's than go up north. I can't stand those people."

"I wish I was going with you," Jasmine lay beside her. "A whole two weeks on the beach!"

"It's not that cool. It's muggy and the mosquitoes can be murderous. I'm just going to be with Grandma. My Grandpa died a few years ago so it's just her and Bean."

Jasmine laughed. "You got an uncle named Bean?"

"No, that's the dog," Amber said as she smiled. "My Grandma is cool. She doesn't care about all this money and stuff. She just loves to be with family."

"Is she poor?"

"Naw, she's got plenty money. She and Grandpa made good money selling their house in Darien then moved into one of those fancy retirement villages on Hilton Head Island."

"What time is your flight leaving?"

"Eight o'clock. Hilton Head doesn't have an airport so I'm flying into Savannah. Javan's going to pick me up there."

Jasmine sat up. "Who's Javan?"

Amber rolled her eyes. "There you go again! Javan is a concierge at the resort where Grandma lives. He's nice."

"I don't care if he's nice; is he fine?"

"Shoot, girl. Javan is a grown man."

"Is he a fine grown man?"

Amber let the smile she'd been holding back emerge. "Mmm hmm! He's chocolate like a Hershey bar with the prettiest eyes I've ever seen on a man."

"What about his body? Does he have a six pack?"

Before Amber could answer, her mother rapped on the door then stuck her head into the room.

"Are you girls in here talking about boys?"

"No Mama, we're talking about men."

Mama frowned. "I bet Jasmine doesn't get smart with her mother, do you Jasmine?"

"No Mrs. Robinson, I don't." Jasmine winked at Amber and Amber sucked her teeth.

"Maybe you can help Amber pack," Mama said.

"Mama!"

Mama held up her hands. "Okay, okay. I'm leaving."

The girls spent the rest of the evening talking. Amber felt melancholy; she and Jasmine would probably never be this close again. She was looking forward to visiting Grandma, but she would miss Jasmine. Then the incident in the bathroom interrupted her thoughts. Her hand went to her necklace. It was cool; unlike the heat she felt when she pinned the goalie to the wall. She dared not talk to Mama about it; she would look at her like she was crazy. But Grandma would understand, or at least she would pretend to. She might even have an answer.

That night Amber didn't dream of hard pack beaches and crashing waves, nor did she dream of her friends and the high school she'd never attend. Instead she dreamed of a gleaming city in the desert, a kingdom nestled in the middle of a lush oasis surrounded by strong and beautiful walls. She dreamed of handsome brown skinned statuesque people; women in loose fitting dresses that fluttered around their athletic bodies, their hands and necks decorated with gold and jewels; men wearing large cotton shirts which covered their loose pants and sporting blue turbans that rested on their heads like crowns, their strong faces bearded and solemn. They lined the edge of a broad avenue which ended before a huge palace occupying the center of the city, its shining towers piercing the azure sky, the pinnacles crowned with indigo flags etched with white woven lions. The people looked at her then to the palace. Amber obeyed their gesture, walking between them to the citadel. She entered the tower to the left where a young girl played among plush rugs with a straw doll, singing a tune that was familiar to Amber's ears. The girl turned then looked at Amber, her face recognizable despite its youth. It was Grandma.

A man entered the room, tall and regal like the people of the streets. A robe fell from his narrow shoulders, the golden fabric filled with sepia colored symbols that moved on their own accord. A single gold band encircled his bald head, its centerpiece a large amber jewel set in gold and surrounded by diamonds. He too, looked at Amber and smiled gently.

"Will you come?" he said. "Will you help us?"

Amber sat up suddenly, flinging her comforter to the floor. She jumped out of bed and ran to the mirror, touching her face. She was real, this was real, but the dream seemed more than real. She searched her memory, wondering why she would dream such a scene. It came back to her slowly; the city was the one that Grandma described to her when she was a child, the city in her stories. She remembered the people as well, strong, beautiful and proud. But Grandma was never in the stories, and neither was the man who spoke to her so clearly. The dream reminded her of the incident in the restroom at the pizzeria. She started to call her mother but stopped. She was a teenager now, thirteen years old. She would handle this herself. She found her iPhone, put on her headphones and listened to Neo. His soulful voice eventually drowned out the images and sang her to sleep.

CHAPTER FOUR

Bagule Fadiki sat on his balcony gazing at the black draped towers of the Sana's palace. He stroked his bearded chin with jewel encrusted fingers, imagining the turmoil of the royal house at the imminent death of their patriarch. He could have summoned a lesser sonchai and asked for a reading, but that would be intrusive. Bagule could be accused of being many things but uncouth was not one of them. He followed the traditions of the kingdom, poured the proper libations to his ancestors, appeared at the required functions and always had a kind word and a generous gift for those less fortunate. He bore no hate for anyone within the walls of Marai and he did nothing covert in his dealings with others. He was an open book and his intentions were obvious. He expected to be the next Sana of Marai, and his first action once the appointment was secure would be to eradicate the barrier between the city and the world beyond the Veil.

Though Bagule was a man of unveiled motives, his enemies were less forthcoming. He was disappointed when Jele Jakada allowed his daughter to escape into the world; her inevitable selection of him as the new Sana would have hastened his rise to power. The possibility existed that she might select someone else but Bagule was prepared for drastic measures. Rumors reached his ears, whispers of the Jele working his schemes again. His spies watched and listened, bringing him words and objects that when pieced together gave him a full picture of Jakada's designs. The Jele had been very busy of late, spending most of his time in his chambers, specifically in his spirit room.

Bagule's thoughts were interrupted by the appearance of Nieleni, his companion. She sauntered to the edge of the balcony wearing a long-layered dress that swished against her ankles, her arms swaying with her hips, her golden bracelets jingling. She grasped the iron railing with her long ring laden fingers, looking in the direction of the palace.

"You obsess," she said.

"Yes, I do," Bagule answered. "I have much to do and the Sana takes too long to die."

Nieleni smiled. She was a beautiful, proper woman born of humble roots, but she had taken to the trappings of nobility quickly.

"I have some information that will please you," she said

Bagule's eyebrow rose as turned to gaze at Nieleni.

"Jakada contacted his daughter," she said. "He has summoned her back to Marai."

Bagule's eyes narrowed as he clasped his hands under his chin.

"She could still select you. Her choice is spiritual."

"Her choice is not certain," Bagule stated. "The elders are more predictable."

"Then you must stop her from returning."

"She lives beyond the Veil. It is forbidden to use nyama outside the city."

Nieleni smirked. "How do you think Jakada contacted her?"

Bagule nodded. "Tradition has been violated. Are you saying I should displease the ancestors as well?"

"If you wish to be Sana, you have no choice."

Bagule went inside, his hands clasped behind his back as he contemplated Nielini's revelation. The only way he could stop Bagule's daughter from returning would be to violate tradition as well. But would that be so wrong? This was a law created by Jele Jakada, decreed by the Sana and upheld by the elders. If Jakada chose to break the rule, then the restriction should not apply to anyone else. Jakada wished the Veil to stay intact and he was willing to break his own law to do so.

"I agree," he finally said. "Something must be done. I will be in my chambers. Gather the talismans and send for my acolytes. I need to know exactly what Jakada is up to."

He walked through his room to the staircase leading to his conjure chambers below his home. He lit the torches, illuminating the altar against the wall opposite the stairs, golden pillars flanking the smooth stone. Piles of gris-gris lined the wall, a spiritual collection of herbs, cloth, bones, and other objects gathered over the years in his quest to influence the elders. Bagule disrobed then stood before the altar in his loincloth, his lean body resembling that of a man much younger than his eight centuries of life. The Veil had that affect, freezing time for everyone under its restriction. He rustled among the gris-gris, selecting the artifacts required for what he was about to do; a ram's horn, a necklace of red and black beads and a small leather pouch containing the hair balls of a lion. He took the enchanted objects to the altar, placing them in the proper pattern. Nieleni entered as he finished, followed by a dozen acolytes. Each person carried a talisman, a powerful object entrusted to them by Bagule. He felt the power; he needed every ounce of it to perform the spell to discover what Jakada was up to.

He gazed upon his acolytes. "Which of you saw Jakada contact his daughter?"

The acolyte stepped forward, a thin man as tall as Bagule with a gaunt, fearful face. Bagule led him to the altar.

"Kneel," he commanded. The acolyte obeyed. Bagule pulled back the man's hood and placed gris-gris on his shoulders. He went to the altar and placed more on the stone. Bagule chanted, waving his hands over the concoction before setting it afire. The others picked up the chant while the fire blazed, consuming the offering and emitting a white smoke that burned the nostrils but heightened the senses. A shape formed within the flames, revealing itself as a kora, a stringed instrument played by jeles as they sang stories and histories. As the fire died Bagule took the kora from the altar then set it aside. He scooped the remaining ashes into a cup holding a milky liquid. He handed the cup to the acolyte.

"Drink."

The acolyte hesitated, but the stern look from his master made him lift the cup to his lips. He was halfway through the potion when he froze, his eyes staring blankly at the altar. Bagule knelt before him, looking deep into his eyes. In the acolyte's eyes he saw images of the days past. He watched Jakada slip into his conjure room and remove a leather shroud from a large mirror. The jele chanted as he waved his hand across the mirror and the image of his daughter appeared. Bagule smiled; she was old, too old to have the nyama to select a new Sana. The smile faded quickly as he followed the conversation. There was a granddaughter, a girl of new womanhood whose powers would be at her peak. They planned to bring her into the city.

Bagule stood and the acolyte collapsed. He was of no more use; the spell would leave him blind.

"Take him to his family," Bagule ordered the other acolytes. "Tell them I will compensate them for his care."

The acolytes lifted the damaged man and left. Nieleni approached with his robe. Bagule dressed then picked up the kora.

"The young one concerns you."

He strummed the kora. Small streams of light danced between the strings, the deep tones reverberating with power.

Bagule smiled in approval. "Yes. We must reach her before Jakada does."

Nieleni's face showed concern. "Will you hurt her?"

Bagule looked at his consort, strumming the kora again. The walls of his chamber hummed and his smile grew wider.

"I will try to prevent her from coming here in time. If I cannot do so then yes, I will hurt her.

CHAPTER FIVE

Amber swayed side to side at the check-in gates of Hartsfield-Jackson International with her backpack and carry-on luggage, an anxious smile on her face. Her Mama looked at her teary-eyed, her father's face disappointed.

"You sure you want to do this, baby girl?" Daddy asked. "Grandma Niecy is going to miss you."

"I'm sure, Daddy," Amber answered. "You know how much I love Hilton Head. Tell Grandma I'll be there soon."

"We should make you go," Mama said. "I'm going to miss my Amby."

Amber's face crinkled at her mother's use of her nickname. "Come on, mom! I'm thirteen!"

"You're just thirteen," her father said. He looked at his Rolex and frowned.

"You best get going now. Your flight leaves in an hour. You sure you know how to get to the gate?"

"Yes, father," she said. "I'll be fine. I have my money and my cell phone and clean underwear."

Her parents laughed and Amber had second thoughts. She really loved both of them, especially when they paid attention to her. Those moments were becoming rare as her father moved up the corporate ladder and her mother's real estate business flourished. They gave her things, good things, but all she wanted was their time. That's why she was going to see Grandma. She wanted to be spoiled with attention and told how much she was loved. Most of all, she just wanted to be herself.

She kissed them both on the cheek then joined the long line leading to the security gates. She looked back as she placed her bags on the scanner; they were still there watching and waving. They waited as she passed through the scanner and approached the escalator leading down to the shuttle, waving until she descended too low to see them. Amber shook her head and grinned.

"Parents."

She turned her attention to the trip. She dug her iPhone out of her purse, put on her earphones then closed off the world, surrounding herself in neo soul heaven. The shuttle dashed to Concourse D, and she joined the rush to exit to the waiting escalator, bobbing her head with the beat. The escalator emerged in the shopping area of the concourse; she looked at her watch then decided to kill some time browsing in the shockingly expensive boutiques. After a few wide eyed moments with outrageous prices, she strolled to her gate and plopped down on the vinyl cushioned seats.

Thirty minutes later she was on a Delta MD 88 headed for Hilton Head Island. She sat next to a white haired balding business man who teased her about going to the island without a set of golf clubs and entertained her with stories of a daughter that was just about her age. The flight attendant paid extra attention to her as well, visiting her seat frequently to see if she was okay. They didn't know she was a veteran traveler; her family's frequent moves because of her father's job and the constant trips with his family made her skilled in the art of above ground travel. She still got a little nervous when the flight got bumpy, but overall flying was routine for her. She didn't tell anyone, though. She loved the attention.

It seemed the jet had just reached cruising altitude when it began its descent to Savannah. By the time they touched down she was giddy, anxious to get to Grandma's and the beach.

Amber waved goodbye to the businessman and the flight attendant as she exited the plane. After a quick jaunt through the terminal she stepped into the humid heat of the Low Country summer, greeted by Javan's handsome smiling face.

"Welcome back, Amber," he said.

"Hey, Javan," she replied in her best attempt to sound mature.

Javan was dressed in the standard Sunrise Resort uniform, white golf shirt with the blue and gold resort emblem on the chest; knee length khaki shorts, knee high white socks and short hiking boots. On the boys at school the uniform would look odd, but on Javan it was perfect. He took her bags and loaded them into the back of the company jeep.

"Your grandmother will be so happy to see you," he said "She's told everyone you're coming."

"I'm glad I'm here. I so didn't want to go to Martha's Vineyard."

Javan looked shocked. "You gave up The Vineyard to come here?"

Amber climbed into the passenger seat. "I know it sounds crazy, but you don't know my Daddy's family. Sometimes I think he must be adopted."

Javan laughed. "Yeah, I know what you mean. My mother's family is the same way. So how long are you going to be with us?"

"Two weeks."

"Wow! I'll have to introduce you to my sister. She's about your age. She can show you what the girls around here do."

"That sounds nice, but Grandma may not be too happy about that. This is her time."

Amber really wasn't interested in meeting his sister. She'd rather spend time getting to know him.

Javan shrugged. "Oh well, maybe next time."

He climbed inside and started the engine.

"Let's go the long way!" she said.

"I don't know, Amber. Your Grandma is anxious to see you."

"Come on, Javan! It's been a long time since I've been here. I've never been over the new bridge."

Javan sighed. "Okay. Let me call your Grandma and let her know we'll be a little late."

Javan called Grandma as Amber settled into her seat. She heard the phone ring.

"Hello Miss Corliss?" Javan said. "Yes ma'am...She's sitting right next to me in the jeep. I'm calling to let you know we're taking the long way through Bluffton...Amber wants to see the new bridge...Yes ma'am."

Javan gave the phone to Amber.

"Hey, Grandma!" Amber exclaimed.

"I thought you came to see me," Grandma said.

"I did! It will only take a few minutes longer."

"I know baby. I was just playing with you. You have fun."

"I will!" She handed Javan his phone and they set off for Hilton Head. They drove through downtown Savannah then over the new suspension bridge leading to South Carolina. The four lanes narrowed to two as they passed through to Hardeeville, crossing tidal creeks and marshland along the way. Amber took in the sights, especially the huge live oaks draped with Spanish moss.

The two-lane road dead-ended at Highway 279, the main thoroughfare to Hilton Head. They took a right turn then sped down the four lanes, passing through the urban congestion of Bluffton, over the curving high rise bridge onto Hilton Head then to the entrance to Sunset Resort. Grandma had certainly announced her arrival; every person they passed waved as they yelled hello. By the time they stopped before Grandma's bungalow Amber felt like a celebrity.

"Here we are, little lady," Javan announced. No sooner had he exited the jeep did the front door open and Grandma emerge with Bean.

"There's my grand baby!" She opened her arms and Amber ran into them, squeezing Grandma Corliss tight.

"Hey Grandma!" she sniffed and smiled. "Ooh, you smell like cookies!"

"I got a batch waiting for you. I hope you're hungry enough to eat them all."

Bean climbed her leg, his tail wagging furiously.

"Get down, boy!" Grandma shouted. "Go on, now!"

"That's okay, Grandma." Amber squatted and hugged the cocker spaniel.

"You been a good boy?" she whispered.

Javan walked up to them loaded down with Amber's luggage. "Where do you want these, Ms. Corliss?"

"Take them back to the guest room." Grandma tugged Amber's arm. "Come on in girl. Javan's going to wait for us. He's going to take us down to the beach."

Amber squealed then covered her mouth, embarrassed that Javan witnessed her child-like outburst. He didn't notice, or at least he didn't let on. She grabbed Grandma's arm and they strolled to the house together.

"Thank you for asking me to come Grandma," she said.

"Shoot, girl, if I had my way you'd live here year 'round. We'll get you in the water then take you over Ms. Lucinda's house and get that hair braided."

Amber dug through her clothes and put on her bathing suit, a royal blue two piece. She stepped out the room and Grandma frowned.

"That thing is a little skimpy, isn't it?" she asked.

Amber did a pirouette. "Me and Mama picked it out. She said I needed a bathing suit for my age."

Grandma shook her head. "Your Mama must think you're thirty, not thirteen. Put something over that until you get in the water."

Amber's shoulders sagged. "Aw, Grandma!"

"You know better than to fuss with me. Go on, now."

Amber went back to her room and returned with her cover up. They met Javan at the jeep and he took them to the trail. Bean jumped out first, running to the beach. Amber ran behind him to the waves and halted, sticking her foot into the water. It was cool but tolerable; she threw off her cover up and high stepped into the waves. This is a vacation, she thought as she plunged into the ocean.

CHAPTER SIX

Corliss spread out her beach blanket and eased down onto the sand. She watched Amber and Bean frolic up and down the beach, Amber's exuberance making what she had to do so much harder. She couldn't remember being so carefree; even at Amber's age she carried the responsibility of being Jele Jakada's daughter and a future seer.

"She's beautiful," her father said.

"You are watching again, I see," Corliss said harshly.

"Yes. I had to see her. Her power is very strong. It will be easy for her to select the next Sana."

Corliss said nothing. She fought to hold back her tears.

"Have you made arrangements?" Jakada asked.

Corliss wiped her cheek, leaving grains of sand below her eye. "Yes. I couldn't get a direct flight. We'll have to fly to Paris and get a connecting flight to Senegal. Cote d' Voire is too dangerous."

"Good. Someone will be waiting for you."

"Who will you send?"

"I will show you tonight."

Corliss didn't notice Amber and Bean running to her until they were almost to the blanket.

"Grandma, have you been crying?"

Corliss wiped her cheek again and sniffed. "Yes, baby, Grandma's been crying. Sometimes when I come out here I get to thinking and it makes me a little sad."

Amber sat beside her as she dried off. "Are you thinking about Grandpa?"

"Yes, baby."

"I know you miss him."

Corliss grasped the towel and dried Amber's hair. "I do, but I'm happy for him, too. He's in a better place."

Amber shrugged. "I can't imagine a better place than this."

Corliss tapped her lightly on the head. "I'm not tolerating any blasphemy, little girl. Remember your Sunday school lessons."

"I'm going back in," Amber announced. "Come on, Bean!"

The two raced back to the waves and plowed in, kicking water and sand high into the air. When they returned Grandma and Amber ate cookies and fed Bean dog biscuits. They stretched out on the blankets and fell asleep in the afternoon sun, safe under the eyes of the resort life guards. When they awoke it was early afternoon, the sun dipping close to the swaying pines and wind bent live oaks. Amber looked at her skin and smiled. She was getting that deep brown color she loved, the skin tone that usually signaled summer. Grandma was awake, staring out into the ocean. She looked at Amber and smiled.

"Worn our already?"

Amber fell back onto the blanket. "Grandma, you just don't know. I hate this private school idea."

"Your parents are trying to do what's best for you," Corliss answered. "Sometimes it's hard to understand when you're young. You'll look back one day and see it was for the best."

Corliss stood. "We best be getting back to the house. I have to start dinner."

Amber smiled. "Mmm mmm! I can taste those biscuits now. Is Javan picking us up?"

Corliss packed their items into the beach basket. "No, baby, I'm feeling good today. We'll walk back."

The three of them strolled down the sidewalk, enjoying the colors of the setting sun. Residents were out as well, taking advantage of the cooling shade.

"Let's play a game, Amber," Corliss announced.

Amber looked skeptical. "It depends, Grandma. I'm a teenager, you know."

Corliss laughed. "I know. I think you'll like this one. I want you to look at my neighbors and tell me about them."

"Tell you what?"

"Anything that comes to mind."

Ralph Thompson sat in a lawn chair in his front yard, a large cigar protruding from his mouth. He nodded hello as he listened to his old radio.

"Let's start with him," Corliss said.

Amber's brows crinkled as she looked at the old man. "He's retired."

They both giggled.

"I know that!" Corliss said. "Tell me something I don't know."

"Okay, here it goes." Amber put her fingers against the side of her head and closed her eyes. "He's sixty-eight, no seventy-one years old. His wife died in her fifties, so he sold their business and retired early. He was one of the first residents of the resort so everyone considers him the old man. He has no children, so he dotes on the young kids that visit the resort. Oh yeah, and he's from up north, New Jersey I think. This is a tropical paradise to him."

Amber opened her eyes ready to share a laugh with Grandma, but Corliss wasn't smiling. Her mouth hung open; a shocked looked in her eyes.

"What's wrong Grandma? Are you alright?"

Corliss blinked her eyes and closed her mouth. "Yes, baby, I'm...uh...I'm fine. Let's try another one."

Amber's eyes narrowed. "I don't know, Grandma."

"Just one more, baby." Corliss searched about and saw Julia Green backing out of her garage in her pink golf cart decorated with daisies.

"Hello, Corliss!" Julia shouted. "Is that your lovely granddaughter?"

"Yes, it is Julia," Corliss shouted back. "She'll be with me for a couple of weeks."

Julia flashed a generous smile. "That's wonderful. You be sure to bring her by before she leaves, okay?"

"Okay!" Corliss waved as Julia sped off.

"Read her," Corliss said.

Amber looked at her nervously. Gone was the playful smile. "Grandma, I'm just making this stuff up," she admitted.

"I know, baby. Just humor your Grandma a little bit longer."

Amber didn't act out like she did the last time. She took a deep breath then stared at Miss Julia for a moment

"Miss Julia came here from Florida after her husband died. She didn't like the year-round warmth, so she moved to Hilton Head to experience the seasons again. She's really not as nice as she seems. She likes to be liked, so she fakes goodness to get attention. She's the kind of person that thinks black people shouldn't be at the resort."

Amber looked at her Grandma. "Are we done now?"

Corliss smiled. "Yes baby; we're done."

They continued to the house in silence, Corliss thoughtful, Amber nervous. Amber went to her room and took a shower while Corliss went to the kitchen to start dinner. Corliss could barely contain herself. Amber had the gift! Her readings were accurate and effortless, and this without any type of training. In Marai she would be praised as a powerful Seer. People would come to her not only in times to select leadership but for any insight to their lives. She would be wealthy and powerful.

Corliss took out the bag of collard greens she had cut up the night before. As she prepared the large cooking pot her mind settled on reality. Yes, Amber would be praised in Marai, but her life would not be her own. She would be wound up in a web of tradition and duty so tight she would suffocate. A leader of Marai was a gilded slave, bound to the traditions and obligated to serve others for the tranquility and prosperity of the city. It was why Corliss fled; now she was sending her granddaughter into the cage she despised.

"She will select the Sana, but she cannot stay," Corliss decided. "She will not stay."

CHAPTER SEVEN

Amber took her time in the shower, her relaxed mood dashed by Grandma's strange behavior during the game. She looked at Amber like the things she said about the neighbors were true. They were made up! She and Jasmine used to play like that all the time, flipping through magazines and making up stories about the lives of the people they saw. As she put on her jeans shorts and Falcons t-shirt a foreboding thought came to her. Maybe Grandma was dying. She remembered how Grandpa changed before he fell sick. It was harder for him to remember things. Sometimes he would just stare at nothing and he didn't know he was doing it. She remembered the day he had the golf cart accident. Grandma wouldn't let him drive after that. Soon afterwards he took sick and died. Tears came to her eyes as she remembered the funeral, the entire family flocked around the burial site, her clutching Mama's hand.

When she came out the room Grandma was standing before the stove with her blue jean apron on, putting the collards into the roiling concoction of water, salt, crushed peppers and fat back. Amber forced away her gloomy thoughts. This was her vacation. Grandma was fine.

"Collard greens? Alright!" Amber exclaimed.

Grandma turned and smiled. "This is why I'm glad you came. I don't get to cook like this that often anymore. This food would sit around until I had to throw it out, but I know my Amber can put down some food."

Amber rubbed her stomach. "Yes I can! Can I help?"

"Of course, baby. You get the rice started while I check on the roast beef."

Amber's eyes grew wide. "Roast beef, too? That's it, I'm staying forever!"

Grandma laughed. "That's the plan!"

Amber took out the burned bottom pot Grandma used for rice and went to work. Together they prepared a tasty dinner of rice, collard greens, roast beef, biscuits and sweet tea. They made their plates and took them into the family room, sitting down before the big screen TV, watching Jeopardy as they savored the meal. After the meal Amber washed dishes as Grandma prepared for bed. Amber changed into her pajamas then met Grandma at the sofa. They talked as they flipped channels, Amber telling Grandma all the details of soccer season, both of them attempting to bury the discoveries and apprehensions of the afternoon. It was close to midnight before they decided to sleep.

Amber brushed Grandma's thick hair, a mane of dark tresses that barely showed grey despite her age. Her thoughts got the better of her and she decided to say something.

"Grandma, you're alright, aren't you?"

Grandma stiffened. "What do you mean?"

Amber continued brushing. "I mean, you're not sick or anything?"

Grandma chuckled. "I'm fine baby."

Amber's hands began to shake. "I had a dream a couple of nights ago. It was about those stories you used to tell me."

Grandma closed her eyes, her face pensive. "What did you dream?"

"I walked through the city. It looked just like you described it, all colorful and filled with high towers. I looked into one of the towers and I saw a girl that looked like you. A man came into the room and he looked like you, too. Or you looked like him; I don't know. Anyway, both of you stared at me as if you could see me. It creeped me out so bad I woke up and couldn't go back to sleep."

"Now why would you dream of Marai?" Grandma asked. "I haven't told you one of those stories for years."

"I know. Maybe I was just missing you."

Grandma smiled. "I miss you too, sugar. That's enough brushing. I think we both need to get some sleep. We'll go to Sea Pines tomorrow and do some dolphin watching."

"Cool!" Amber put down the brush and kissed Grandma on the cheek. "Good night, Grandma."

Grandma kissed her back. "Good night, baby."

She was headed for bed when the incident came to her.

"Grandma, there's something else. Actually, a couple of things."

"What is it, baby?"

She trudged back to the bed then snuggled against Grandma.

"Ooh, this must be bad," Grandma said.

"You know how you told me not to wrestle unless it was absolutely necessary?"

Grandma pulled away from her. "What did you do, Amber?"

"Well, there were these girls from the other team that decided to get back at me in the rest room at the pizza place. I had to kind of put them in their place."

"You didn't hurt them, did you?"

"Their feelings but that's all," she said.

"That doesn't sound so bad," Grandma said.

"Well, here's the thing," Amber said. "One of the girls was coming at me and I held my hand out to tell her to stop. My necklace got warm and she lifted off her feet then slammed into the bathroom door."

Amber felt Grandma stiffen.

"You sure that's what you saw?" Grandma asked.

Amber nodded. "I only told you because Mama and Daddy would think I was crazy."

"I think it's time for bed," Grandma said.

"Really?"

"Yeah, baby girl. Grandma has some thinking to do."

Amber got out of the bed. "Good night, Grandma."

"Good night sugar."

As Amber walked to her room she grinned. Something was going on, and Grandma knew about it.

* * *

Guilt kept Corliss awake as she tried to find a way to spare Amber her duty.

"She must come to us," her father's voice intruded. "You should have told her today."

"I gave her one more day of innocence," Corliss said. "She has the rest of her life to be a Seer."

"You will tell her tomorrow?" Her father's voice sounded unsure.

"I will," Corliss replied. "Tomorrow she will be yours."

CHAPTER EIGHT

Jakada watched Alake a few moments more after she slept, fighting the remorse causing him to question his decision. Amber's life would change, but so does everyone's, sooner or later. Her responsibility would be much greater than most, but that was inconsequential. Soon she would be a woman and would have to become a responsible person in the world outside. It was no different than Marai.

He shifted from Alake's mirror to his great granddaughter's. Amber slept soundly, her earphones barely on her head as the sound of her music whispered into the night. Such a beautiful girl, he thought. She would be well accepted in the city and her decision would be final. But she could not stay. For her sake he worked on an elixir that would alter her memory of the event. He did this for Alake, for otherwise Amber would not be allowed to leave Marai once she entered. The new Sana was sure to uphold the separation of the city from the world, for he or she would be wise enough and pious enough to understand the need. In other words, the new Sana would be nothing like Bagule.

He looked into the evening sky, finding comfort in the familiar constellations before leaving his tower. His footfalls echoed off the compound walls, the streets desolate save a wandering dog or goat. Most people were in the farmlands surrounding the city, taking advantage of the bright full moonand spending extra hours in their fields. Jakada had an appointment with the Margara, the Sana's great wife. She was anxious to hear about Amber. Tradition dictated that the Margara become the wife of the next Sana. She would be a symbolic wife only, a representation of the past rule supporting the reign of a new leader. Jakada knew the possibility of being betrothed to Bagule sickened her, symbolic or otherwise.

The palace guards made way for Jakada without hesitation. The wide courtyard was lit with torches perched on the inner wall, their flickering light adding movement to the moon's luminescence. At the far end of the wall, before the palace entrance, the Margara sat under a canopy of woven grass, flanked by a host of bodyguards. Her djele stood beside her, his face noncommittal as always. The Margara smiled as Jakada approached, her beauty still vibrant after so many years. He advanced the appropriate distance then fell to his knees, touching his head to the ground.

"Margara, I come with news," he announced.

"Approach, uncle," she replied, honoring him with her response.

Jakada approached the queen, his back bent so as not to rise above her height.

"What do you have to tell me, Jakada?"

"The Seer has been found. She will be here soon."

Margara frowned. "Why is she not here now?"

"These matters are delicate, Margara. The new Seer has been raised with no knowledge of us or our ways. My daughter will have to inform her of her duty and make sure she is willing to come and make the selection."

"This is ridiculous!" the Margara howled. "If you sent your daughter away to protect her you have failed not only as a father but as a warrior. The Sana is hours away from death, days at the most."

The Margara ceased talking; she trembled as tears formed at the corners of her eyes.

"All will be well, Margara," Jakada assured. "She has the sight. When Alake tells her about us she will believe because she will sense Alake is telling the truth."

"How will she come to us?"

"They will fly to Paris...."

The Margara frowned. "Fly? What do you mean fly? And what is this Paris?"

"They will fly as in come swiftly," Jakada said. "As for Paris, it is a city to the north, in Bukraland."

The Margara's expression made it obvious she still did not understand but she moved on.

"You have taken precautions?"

"Of course."

The Margara was silent, her eyes moving as if she was searching for something else to say.

"We do not have to speak," Jakada said. "I can wait until you have something else you wish to know."

The Margara's shoulders slumped as she tilted her head away from Jakada. "I don't want to go back in there, Jakada," she confessed. "I love him, but I hate seeing him like this. I fear this will be my lasting memory of him and I don't want that."

"It is his time," Jakada said. "The Sana has lived a long and prosperous life. The ancestors wish his presence now."

"The ancestors must be blind to the consequences of their selfishness," she snapped. "I need...we need him here. Our world will change if..."

"Do not worry," Jakada said. "Alake will not fail us."

The Margara sat straight; her posture signaling her moment of personal grief was over.

"What if Bagule doesn't accept the judgment? What if he rebels?"

"Then I will deal with him," Jakada replied.

"I will trust you, Jakada," she finally said. "You have been a loyal servant of the Sana, but most of all you have been a friend. I know you will not lead us down the wrong path. You may go."

Jakada walked backwards until he was the customary distance from the Margara. He knelt, remaining so until the Margara and her entourage entered the palace. He heard the exaggerated slam of the door then stood to leave. As he walked away he was unnerved by the Margara's anxiety. She feared Bagule's power and rightfully so.

Jakada would have to make sure Alake and Amber arrived at Marai safely.

He called for Kamba once he returned to his tower.

"Bring Bissau to me immediately," he ordered.

The tall man bowed then hurried away, his destination the nyama apprentice school. As Jakada paced in his parlor he contemplated his decision. He was about to put another person in harm's way, risking another life to correct a mistake made long ago. At least Bissau was skilled; he was the best candidate for his plan.

The servant appeared at his door. "Sir, Bissau is here."

He stepped aside and Bissau entered the room. For a boy just recently initiated into manhood, Bissau carried himself with the confidence of men twice his age. He was tall for his age as well, sporting a wide frame that promised the body of a warrior in years to come. With skin like the night and a smile like the stars, Bissau was admired by men and women but showed no sign of the vanity that usually afflicted such people. Bissau was also steeped in nyama. Jakada realized this early and took the boy into apprenticeship. The boy excelled beyond anyone's expectations while remaining humble and respectful. He was a boy that if not for his bloodline would make an excellent Sana.

"What can I do for you, Jele Jakada?" he asked.

"I have a task for you Bissau, a very important one."

Bissau's smile grew wide and Jakada frowned.

"Don't be so eager," he warned. "You don't know the details."

"I am sure whatever you have for me will be an adventure, jele."

Jakada sat on his stool. "That it will. I need you to go on a journey to retrieve something very valuable to me."

"Where must I go, Jele?"

"Paris."

Bissau looked confused. "Paris? I do not know this Paris, Jele. Is this a new district in the city?"

"No Bissau, Paris is not in Marai. Paris is a city beyond our city. It is a city beyond the Veil."

Bissau's mouth dropped open and Jakada smiled.

"I told you not to be so anxious."

Bissau sat on the floor before Jakada. "Forgive me, Jele. I thought it was forbidden for anyone to go beyond the Veil."

"It was I who created the Veil," Jakada answered. "And it was I who urged the Sana to create such a law. I was also the first person to violate his law, for I allowed my daughter to pass through in order to protect her from Bagule. Now she needs to return and she needs my help. She needs our help."

Bissau gazed at his sandaled feet for a moment. "If you think this must be done, then who am I to argue? You have always favored me Jele, even when I did not deserve it. You have never led me wrong. What must I do?"

"We haven't much time. The world beyond the Veil is much different from ours. The things you see will astound you, but you must remain focused."

Jakada stood and motioned for Bissau to follow. He led the apprentice to his room containing the mirror.

"You will stay in this room and study the images that appear before you. I will try to answer any questions you have, but I must admit my knowledge of these people is sparse. We will wait to hear from my daughter before we proceed further."

Bissau nodded in agreement. "I will do as you ask Jele. I will bring your daughter and great granddaughter home."

"I hope so, Bissau. I hope so."

CHAPTER NINE

The acolyte collapsed to the floor convulsing, blood streaming from his nose, ears and eyes. The others tried to calm him, pressing cool wet cloths to his head and chanting spells to ease his spirit. Their efforts were in vain. The man rose as if attempting to stand then collapsed again. He was dead.

"Take him away," Bagule ordered with the flip of his hand. The acolytes removed their brother, cutting fearful glances at their master. They were there to serve him, but lately serving the whims of the mage had costs some of them their lives.

Bagule sensed the uneasiness of his servants but he could not bend to sympathy. It was essential he knew everything occurring in Jakada's tower and the only way to do so was to use spies. The jele took much care protecting his motives from magical eyes, so Bagule resorted to more conventional means. He saw through the eyes of others. The information was worth the price.

He strolled to his lounging chair, picking up his kora on the way. The girl unnerved him. She was a more of a threat than Alake ever was or ever would be. She read two people with no training and she wasn't even aware of it.

He strummed a simple tune as Nieleni entered the conjure chambers. She halted at the door and waited. Bagule sat down the instrument then nodded for her to approach.

"Were you able to acquire her services?" he asked.

"Yes, but she was very expensive."

Bagule waved his hand. "Gold is of no consequence. Where is she?"

"She is waiting in your study."

Bagule rushed from the chambers, climbing the steps to his study with long strides as Nieleni ran to keep pace. They entered his study and the woman stood. She was nearly as tall as Bagule with the dark brown skin common to her people. Her eyes radiated with the color of gold. She wore a vibrant dress of red, yellow and blue, her necklaces crowding around her long regal neck. Bracelets pushed against her wrists and a broad beaded belt holding a curved dagger gripped her slender waist. She smiled and nodded as Bagule entered the room, the most acknowledgement of his station she would give. In her land she was an equal to the conjurer.

"Aisha, I'm glad you agreed to help me."

"I'm surprised you accepted my price," Aisha replied, her voice child-like.

"Desperate times require desperate measures. I assume you are aware of my dilemma?"

"Yes, I am," she replied. "When do you wish me to leave?"

"As soon as possible." Bagule congratulated himself for thinking of this plan. He would be able to thwart Jakada without violating the rules established hundreds of years ago. The law clearly stated no Maraibu could leave the city, but Aisha was not Maraibu. She was like nothing anyone had ever seen.

"Deposit my payment with my banker," she said, handing him a folded piece of parchment. "Don't try to rob me. I can be vengeful."

"Everyone in Marai knows me as an honest man,' Bagule replied. "Your money is safe."

"Then I am off to Paris!" The woman sat on the floor. She closed her eyes and began to transform before Bagule's eyes. He had seen her perform many times and still the transformation fascinated him. Most left the theaters trying to decipher the elaborate trickery, but Bagule knew it was real. Aisha was a shape shifter, a person possessing the nyama to be anything at any time. Even calling her a woman was a stretch, because a true shaper shifter like Aisha could change gender as well. When she was done a jackal stood before him, a dark brown canine with golden eyes wearing a golden necklace. It barked and ran by him to the tower steps, heading for the gates of the city. Bagule watched her run through the night streets, reaching the wall ramparts in moments then leaping towards the Veil. For a moment he thought it would stop her but she passed through without effort. As she landed on the sand she transformed again, growing to the shape of a camel, the only constant her glowing golden eyes. He returned to his study then played his kora. Soon we will all be able to do just as you, he thought. Soon we will all be free.

CHAPTER TEN

Amber awoke to the sound of the morning news and the smell of sausages and pancakes. She dragged herself into the kitchen just as Grandma placed a plate stacked with steaming hot pancakes on the table. Fat hotel sausages hung on the edge of the plate.

"Morning, Grandma," she croaked.

"Hey baby! Breakfast is ready."

Amber sat at the table, picked up her knife and fork then cut her pancakes into small cubes. She yawned as she picked up the pure maple syrup bottle Grandma always served then drenched her pancake squares.

"I'm glad you're taking me shopping today Grandma," Amber said. "I'm eating my way out of my clothes."

Grandma looked at Amber and shook her head. "What are you talking about? You look like you been on a prison diet. I'm just trying to put some meat on them bones."

"Please stop, Grandma," Amber mumbled, her mouth filled with pancake. "I can't take it!"

"So stop eating."

"Not a chance!"

Javan met them later that morning, his ever-present smile adding to the bright warm sunshine. They loaded into the jeep then traveled to Shelter Cove, where Grandma spent way too much money on a few items that Amber loved but was afraid to ask for. The next stop was Sea Pines for a leisurely lunch in Harbor Town and souvenir shopping. Amber bought a few more shells to add to her collection and a big stuffed starfish to give to Jasmine as a joke. From there they rode bikes to the South Marina, where to Amber's delight the ice cream shop was still selling the hot brownies and ice cream with chocolate topping she loved so much. After a quick jaunt to Beaufort for a few special groceries they were back at Sea Pines, catching a local cruise for a sunset dinner and dolphin watching.

Amber leaned over the side of the boat, scanning the waterways for dolphin fins. She saw a grey image break the surface and jumped up and down.

"Grandma, look! I see one!"

Amber searched but couldn't find Grandma. She walked to the bow and found Grandma sitting near the railing. She gazed into the distance, tear tracks on her cheeks. Amber hurried to her side.

"Grandma, what's wrong?"

Grandma looked into Amber's eyes and smiled. "Nothing, baby. I was just thinking that's all."

Amber mustered up her strength, squeezing Grandma's hand tight.

"Grandma, are you dying?"

Grandma kissed her cheek. "No, baby, Grandma isn't going anywhere just yet. But you and I need to have an important conversation."

Amber was confused. What would Grandma need to talk to her about that was so important? She had the required womanhood conversation with her mom, which was embarrassing, and her dad, which was downright creepy. She was sure Grandma had nothing to add to those discussions.

Grandma seemed to sense her confusion. "Don't worry, baby. It will be alright. We'll talk tonight."

The cruise lasted two hours but Amber couldn't relax. She kept trying to figure out what Grandma wanted to discuss that was so important. Maybe she wasn't dying but wanted to talk about her will. Amber frowned; that was another conversation she didn't want to have. Besides, that was a discussion for Mama, not her. Maybe she wanted to set her straight about Javan. That thought made her smile. She thought Javan was the perfect man, but she was realistic. She was thirteen; Javan was at least twenty, practically an old man. Every boy she met was held to his standards and so far all of them failed. Now when she turned twenty-one, Javan would be twenty-eight; that wasn't so bad if she could just hold out.

She giggled; she was thinking like Jasmine. The thought lightened her mood though, so she sat back and enjoyed the setting sun over the marshlands, barely anticipating the talk with Grandma later that evening.

She was tired by the time they settled in at the bungalow but she refused to fall asleep. Grandma seemed to be dragging it out, puttering around the kitchen and doing all kinds of little things as she avoided Amber's questioning eyes. Finally, at almost midnight, Grandma called Amber to her room.

She lay in her bed, her hair resting on her shoulders and Bean in her arms. She stroked the dog absently, her eyes settling on Amber as she entered the room. Amber sat at the foot of the bed, blinking her eyes as she wrung her hands.

"Yes, Grandma?"

"What I'm about to tell you I've never told anyone, not your mother, your grandfather, anyone."

Amber leaned in closer. "What is it, Grandma?"

Grandma cleared her throat. "I am not from here. I'm from Africa."

"Africa's a big continent Grandma," Amber replied.

Grandma grinned. "These days the land is called Chad. When I lived there it had no name, for no country existed. The land was divided among city-states controlling the trade routes between the north and the south. There were many cities, but my home was the greatest of all."

There was something familiar about Grandma's confession. It didn't take long for Amber to figure out what.

"This sounds just like the stories you used to tell me."

58

Grandma's expression became serious. "Those were not stories, Amber. Everything I told you was the truth. I was telling you about my life."

Amber sat stunned. "Those were fairy tales, Grandma. Gleaming cities, magic people..." She smiled. "Quit playing with me, Grandma."

"She tells the truth," a man's voice said from behind her.

Amber jumped to her feet then scurried to the head of Grandma's bed. She turned to see the man from her dream in Grandma's dresser mirror. He wore a loose fitting white shirt that draped to his knees, covering most of his pants. A white beaded necklace circled his neck and a golden band rested on his clean-shaven head. He bowed slightly and smiled.

"Amber, this is your great-grandfather Jakada, Grand Jele of Marai," Grandma said.

"Hello Amber," Jakada said.

Amber's eye shot back and forth between the image in the mirror and her grandmother's serene smile.

"This is crazy," she managed to say. "Grandma, this isn't funny anymore. Stop it."

"You know this is real," Jakada said. "Look into your grandmother like you did her neighbors and you'll see the truth."

"But that was a game!" Amber protested.

"Everything you said was true," Grandma said. "The game was a test to see if you possessed the gift."

Amber reached her hands out to steady herself. "Okay, okay, this is enough. I want to go home, Grandma. I want to go home now!"

"Baby, look at me," Grandma said.

Amber cut a suspicious glance at Grandma. "Why?"

"Just look at me."

Amber stared into Grandma's eyes. A feeling of calm overcame her as a procession of images flooded her mind. Verdant savanna appeared, teeming with antelopes, giraffes, elephants and other creatures familiar to the African continent. Moments later a small group of people entered from the south, settling near a winding river then building a collection of conical huts. The village expanded quickly, transforming from huts to homes to tower compounds encased by brightly colored walls and separated by wide avenues. She watched fascinated as a grand wall rose around the compounds, becoming the boundary of what was now a thriving city. Her view narrowed as she soared over the city streets, watching the grandeur of the city increase as she drew nearer to its heart. Then she followed a young girl in a bright blue dress and bouncing braids running into a grand tower then into the arms of a man who lifted her high. They turned to face her; it was Grandma and her father.

Amber shook her head and the image faded. Her grandmother could be tricking her; this man in the mirror might just be a hoax or a swindler. No, she decided. Grandma was telling the truth and so was this man who claimed to be her great-grandfather. She returned to the bed, curling up against Grandma but keeping her eyes on Grandma's father.

"Why did you leave?" Amber asked Grandma.

Grandma sighed. "I was young. I didn't want the responsibility of my position. I wanted to be like the children I saw in the market place, running free and playing with no thought of their future. I knew I could never have that type of life in Marai, so I stole my father's Key and escaped the city. Or so I thought."

"Alake's life was in danger," Jakada continued.

"Alake?" Amber's was confused. "Who is Alake?"

"That is my name," Grandma explained. "It is my oriki, my pet name used only by those close to me."

"Your grandmother was destined to select the next Sana," her great grandfather continued. "Even when she was young it was common knowledge that the Sana was seeing his final days. There were those that wished to take his place but knew she would not select them for their hearts were not true. If she was eliminated the task would fall on the Elders' council. Many of the Elders have loyalties that have nothing to do with choosing the best Sana."

"The time has come to choose a new Sana," Grandma said. "This may not mean much to you and the people of this world, but to the Maraibu this is the most important of decisions. It rests in your hands."

"Grandma I don't know," Amber said. "What if I choose the wrong person?"

"You won't," Grandma replied. "It's not possible. The Seer always makes the right choice."

"But we have to go to Africa, I mean Marai. What are we going to tell Mama and Daddy?"

"We won't tell them anything," Grandma answered. "I have the plane tickets and you have new clothes. We can be there and back before summer break is over."

"What if I don't want to do it?" Amber finally said. "What if I don't want to go?"

Grandma looked at her father and his smile faded.

"It is your decision, Amber," he answered. "I cannot force it upon you. If I had been wiser we would not need you. If you refuse we will speak no more of this. I will make you forget this conversation ever occurred. But you must know what your decision will beget. If you do not select the next Sana a council of elders will do so. They will select a man named Bagule, a powerful man who had vowed to lift the Veil between Marai and the world. Your world will suffer far beyond anything you can imagine if this happens."

Amber looked at her grandmother for help and she smiled.

"You know what he says is true," she said. "You see it in his heart."

"We'll be back before Mama and Daddy knows?"

Jakada's face brightened. "Yes."

Amber took Grandma's hand. "I'll do it."

CHAPTER ELEVEN

Aisha the camel sauntered into the Tuareg camp just before dawn so as not to be seen. She cursed herself for her ill luck; the Tuaregs valued camels more than anything. If she was seen the herders would know immediately she did not belong to them. They would fight over her and eventually she would go with the man with the most gold. She scanned the camp and was disappointed. The fortunes of these proud desert folks had apparently diminished since the last time she'd been among them, which had to be at least three centuries ago. Still, they would get her where she needed to go.

She worked her way to the middle of the herd before transforming. The back pack she carried lay at her feet; she dressed quickly then snuck into the camp. Another quick scan told her she was the only woman in the camp, which could pose an issue. She had no worries about her safety for she was a trained fighter and had bested many men in armed and unarmed combat. Her main concern was the oddity of her arrival. Aisha shrugged; there was no way she could avoid an unusual situation. She might as well be quick about it.

"Wake up you lazy goat herders!" she shouted.

Men stumbled out of their tents, clearing their eyes to the image of a beautiful but apparently crazy woman dressed in odd looking clothes and screaming too loud too early in the morning. One of the men, a tall, lanky fellow covered in a light blue robe and a dark blue shesh approached her with angry eyes.

"Who are you, sister? Why are you disturbing our sleep?"

"I need to go to Paris," she replied. "Can you take me there?"

"Take you…to Paris?" The man laughed. "You are a mad woman! How did you get here?"

"I did not come here to discuss my circumstances," Aisha replied. "I came here to get to Paris." She reached into her bag and pulled out three large gold nuggets. "Is this enough to get me there?"

The man's eyes widened. "Praise to Allah! Where did you get that?"

"You ask too many questions and answer none, goat herder. Can you take me to Paris?"

The man bowed. "Of course I can. We can leave immediately."

He reached for the gold but Aisha snatched it away. Before the man could protest Aisha held a dagger at this throat.

"Don't play with me, goat herder," she hissed. "I sting like a scorpion."

"I am a man of my word," he replied. "I will get you to Paris."

Aisha flashed a confident smile. "Good. Which camels are yours?"

The man laughed. "We're not taking the camels! That will take too long, and camels can't get you to Paris. My men are heading north for salt. If you wish to go to Paris we have to go south. We're taking the truck."

Aisha nodded, careful not to reveal her confusion. What is a truck? she thought.

The man turned away then cupped his hands around his covered mouth.

"Taleeb! Bring the truck!"

The answer approached her rumbling like a storm and smoking like a dung fire. It looked like a wagon without horses. She was fascinated but not surprised; over the years she had seen the ingenuity of man. The truck approached them then stopped. The door swung open and Taleeb climbed out. The man patted Taleeb's shoulder.

"Make sure you get a good exchange. I will meet you here in a month."

Aisha watched the man climb inside. She went to the opposite side and repeated his gestures, grinning triumphantly when the door opened. She climbed in and sat on the comfortable seat.

"By the way, my name is Busari," the man said.

"I prefer goat herder," Aisha replied.

"There is no need to insult me," Busari argued. "What is your name?"

"Aisha," she said. "Can we go now?"

They traveled south at a speed Aisha never thought capable of anything other than birds in flight. In a half a day they had covered the distance of a month on camel back. Her perfect smile grew so wide her jaws hurt. At this rate she would be in Paris in days.

They camped overnight, Busari sharing his targuella with her. Aisha bit into the bread with relish. She had always savored desert food for its flavor and simplicity. Her meals in Marai were sumptuous but wasteful. She slept that night with a content stomach.

The next morning, they continued on. Aisha tried to keep conversation between her and Busari to a minimum, but one question would not leave her be until she asked it.

"Why do you use camels to transport your salt when you have this truck?"

"The truck is much faster I will admit, but the camels carry more salt without breaking it," Busari replied. "I have only one truck but many camels. One day I will have enough money to buy a fleet of trucks." He patted his bag. "Your payment is a good start."

Aisha cursed under her breath. She had paid him too much. She would have to be more observant once they reached Paris. She didn't want to draw too much attention.

A small village appeared on the horizon as they made the transition from desert to the grassland of the Sahel. A paved road appeared from under the sand and the ride became much smoother and faster.

"Is this Paris?" she asked.

Busari laughed. "Of course not, crazy woman! This is Gosi. I have a friend here that will take you to Senegal. From there you can catch a flight to Paris. You do have enough money to take you to Paris, don't you?"

"Of course," Aisha snapped. She had no idea how much money it would take to get to Paris, nor did she comprehend his use of the phrase 'catching a flight'.

They continued into Gosi, finally stopping at a mud-brick building in the center of town. A dark man in billowing khaki pants and a sweat stained white shirt came out to greet them.

"Busari, what are you doing here?" the man said. "I thought you'd be half way across the desert by now."

"I was until I met this crazy woman," he answered. "She wants to go to Paris but she doesn't know where it is."

The man helped Aisha from the truck. "I am Amadou. Why does my friend call you crazy?"

"Your friend is rude and stupid," Aisha said. "I am Aisha. I wish to go to Paris. Can you take me there?"

Amadou laughed. "I think you are touched, Madame Aisha. I can fly you as far as Dakar. You can take Air France from there. You do have a passport, don't you?"

"Of course I do." Aisha had no idea what a passport was.

Amadou was more observant than Busari. "I have friends that can get you a passport. All this will be expensive; very expensive."

Aisha reached into her bag and extracted more gold, considerably less than she offered Busari. Amadou's eyes gleamed.

"You are heaven sent, Madame Aisha! I will make the arrangements immediately."

Busari nodded. "You are in excellent hands. Amadou will take care of you. He's an honest man and a good friend. I must get back to my salt. Good luck Aisha the crazy woman!"

Busari jumped into his truck and sped away amid a cloud of sand. Aisha followed Amadou inside the mud brick building. The air was incredibly cool despite the outside heat. She wrapped her arms around herself and shivered.

"Great, isn't it?" Amadou said proudly. "I have the only working air conditioner in Gosi." He went to a large white box across the room and opened it. He took out a bottle filled with a brown liquid, twisting the top to open it.

"I have the only working refrigerator as well," he said as he handed her the bottle.

Aisha eyed it suspiciously and drank. Cool sweetness exploded in her mouth, followed by a slight burning sensation. She burped unexpectedly. Whatever this elixir was, she was totally in love with it. She sat calmly and waited, dazzled by the wonders surrounding her. Amadou held what looked like a small box to his ear and talked, stopping now and then to smile at her. He finally took the box down.

"My friends are awaiting our arrival. If we leave now we should reach Dakar by nightfall."

Amadou strode out of the building and Aisha followed. They boarded another thing that looked like a truck only smaller. They sped across town to an open field. Another strange thing sat in the middle of the area. Aisha felt nervous and took another swig of the incredibly good elixir.

Amadou stepped out of the vehicle then patted her shoulder as he walked by. "Come on! My friends are waiting for us."

They approached the thing and Amadou opened the door.

"How do you like my plane? It's the only one in Gobi."

"It's...beautiful?" Aisha said.

She sat in the soft cushions. Amadou sat on the other seat behind a wheel that looked similar to the one Busari used to guide the truck. Aisha relaxed a bit. Whatever she was in must be some type of vehicle similar to the truck.

Amadou reached over her and she struck him on the head.

"Ow!" He leaned away rubbing his scalp. "I was trying to buckle your seat belt. It can be tricky."

"I can do it myself," Aisha looked at the belt buckle and was totally confused.

"Go ahead," she said. "But ask permission the next time."

Amadou reached across Aisha gingerly and buckled her in. He turned a key on the panel before him and the blades before the truck began spinning. Aisha was so fascinated it took her a moment to realize they were moving. The craft built up speed…then began lifting off the ground. Terror filled Aisha's eyes despite her attempt to hide it.

Amadou looked at her and laughed. "Your first time flying, huh?"

Aisha nodded her head and drank more elixir.

"I'm not surprised. Most desert folk have never been up in a plane. As a matter of fact, there's still quite a few that have never seen one. This is a little bugger. The plane taking you to Paris will be much bigger."

Aisha sank into her seat, clutching her almost empty elixir bottle. This trip was going to be more than she expected, much more.

CHAPTER TWELVE

Bissau locked himself away in Jakada's spirit room for a week, studying the images flashing across the enchanted mirror surface. In the beginning he was overwhelmed, struggling to comprehend the world beyond and its difference. Eventually the newness waned and he began to learn. The world beyond the Veil was much more advanced than Marai in many ways, but in other ways it was woefully deprived. He was especially upset when he observed the conditions of the lands surrounding the city. The people suffered needlessly because of the greed and abuse of others. The ancestors taught them of the natural hierarchy, how some were blessed with more nyama and naturally prospered more in worldly endeavors. But they also taught that those with more were obligated to help those with less. That lesson was conveniently forgotten by the people beyond the Veil.

He was immersed in the images of Paris when Jakada entered the room.

"Are you ready, Bissau?"

The young man stood. "Yes, Jele, I am ready." Bissau was dressed in the best imitation of Parisian fashion Jakada's tailors could produce. He carried a leather backpack, a beautiful creation of Marai design filled with the talismans and gris-gris he would need for the journey. Jakada inspected him and smiled.

"You are ready," he said. "I wish I could have supplied you with everything you need, but some items are beyond our abilities. Alake has given me the details of the inn where she and Amber will be waiting. Once you locate them you must bring them to the mirror and I can transport you all here."

"Where will this mirror take me, Jele?" Bissau asked.

"I don't know," Jakada admitted. "This is where the adventure begins."

Jakada stepped past Bissau and waved his hand across the mirror. The streaming images dissipated, replaced by a black void. The jele turned to his apprentice and smiled.

"The ancestors are with you," he said. "You will bring them back."

Bissau bowed to Jakada, took a deep breath and stepped into the void. He was engulfed in blackness, his skin tingling with strange sensations. He floated, his feet searching for a surface to stand on, his hands reaching forward for something to grasp. Then suddenly he was falling, tumbling though the darkness. His fall ended abruptly against a wooden floor. He hesitated then fell again as the crumbling floor gave way. His second landing was more abrupt and painful. Bissau lay still, gathering himself and regaining his breath. He looked up through the hole he created, the jagged ends of the broken boards outlined by the dim moonlight.

Bissau struggled to a sitting position. The dilapidated building was empty, which was good. He should have no problem bringing Alake and Amber back for the return to Marai. He had no idea how they would get back to the portal, but he would solve that problem later. He needed to get his bearings.

He tried to stand. Pain stabbed his shoulder and he instinctively grabbed it. He closed his eyes and probed the area with his fingers. He was relieved; nothing was broken, but it was severely bruised. Healing could wait until he was on his way.

It took him a moment to find his way out of the structure. He stood alone, surrounded by an overgrown field resembling an oasis thick with trees, shrubs, grass and sheep. Marai's pastures were sparse in comparison. He had no time to marvel; he needed to find out where he was so he could set off to Paris. He saw lights to the north, or what he assumed was north, a sign of life. Bissau ambled up the road, gravel crunching beneath his boots. The damp air made it hard to breath and he tired quickly. He would adapt soon, he suspected, but until then he was not very fond of this place called France.

He finally reached the farmhouse and knocked on the door.

"Who is it?" a man's voice demanded.

"Excuse me, monsieur," Bissau said in heavily accented French. "I am lost and I need your help."

The door opened and a huge man stepped out. A thick beard covered his face, his pale skin almost sickly to Bissau's eyes. He looked at the apprentice with disapproval.

"You're a long way from Paris, African," the man snarled.

Bissau's eyes widened. He thought he landed in Paris.

"I'm sorry to disturb you, sir, but I am looking to return to Paris. I fell in with the wrong type and they left me stranded."

"I don't blame them," the man replied. "Your kind has made a mess of France. The closest train station is in Crecy. I suggest you go immediately."

There was no chance this man would let him stay the night.

"Merci, monsieur," Bissau said. He left quickly, following the road in the direction the man pointed. He turned back and the man was still on the porch glaring. Bissau stopped and opened his bag. He took out his wrist knives and put them on. The look in the man eyes suggested he might need them. He planned to avoid trouble, but he definitely wasn't going to run from it, especially out in the countryside. He had been walking for an hour before he saw the lights coming up behind him. A bad feeling swept over him; he moved closer the road's edge, hoping to reach the woods before the lights reached him. He thought of running, but if whoever carried the lights caught up to him before he reached the woods he would be too tired to defend himself. So he walked, using his ears to keep up with the closing vehicle. The vehicle pulled up beside him and stopped suddenly. Three men jumped out; the driver was the big angry Frenchman.

"See, I told you," the big man said. "This is the African that tried to break in my house!"

One of the men, a young man with blond hair and red cheeks, looked at Bissau skeptically. "We should call the police, Pierre."

"We don't need the police," Pierre sneered. "We can handle this monkey ourselves."

"Please," Bissau said as he raised his hands. "I meant no harm. I was just trying to get to Paris."

"Liar!" The big man rushed him. Bissau waited until his attacker was almost on him before stepping aside. Pierre stopped just short of stumbling into the woods.

The third man, tall and lanky with wheat colored hair and a thin face, tried to grab Bissau but the apprentice slapped his hand away. He snarled then swung at Bissau's head. Bissau ducked and hit the man in the chest with his open hand, knocking the wind out of him. He crumpled to the street gasping. Bissau heard shuffling feet and spun to see Pierre charging him again. Bissau dropped low and spun, whipping out his left leg and kicking Pierre's feet from under him. Pierre crashed onto his side, his head striking the pavement hard, knocking him unconscious.

Bissau kept spinning as he stood to face the skeptical friend. The man backed away.

"Don't touch me," he said. "I have no argument with you."

An idea came to his head. "Is this your automobile?"

"No, it's Pierre's."

"Can you take me to Paris? I will pay you."

The man looked at his friends writhing on the ground. "I can't just leave them here. They are my friends."

"Your friends attacked me for no reason. I could have hurt them much worse, but I didn't. You can make amends by taking me to Paris. I think they can find their way home from here."

The Frenchman looked at his friends and frowned. "Get in."

Bissau smiled. "Thank you."

"Don't thank me. I don't want to be responsible for what might happen once Pierre tells everyone else about you. I will take you to Paris but you must promise never to return."

"I promise," Bissau lied. He would have to return to pass through the mirror. But he would worry about that later. Tonight, he was on his way to Paris.

CHAPTER THIRTEEN

Amber awoke the next morning to an impatient sun stealing through the slits of her blinds. She remained still, looking around her room with sleepy eyes. She had no illusions about the night before; everything that happened in Grandma's room was real. So many questions ran through her head, questions she would have to have answered. The responses wouldn't change her decision, but they would make her feel better about what she was going to do.

She forced herself out of bed to the closet where she began to pack. Grandma bought her a new wardrobe for the trip; most of the items were still in packages. She placed them into the new suitcases and combined them with her old items. She wasn't a heavy packer; her mother always complained she never had enough clothes whenever they travelled. She had no idea what the weather would be in Paris this time of year, let alone West Africa. She would have to search it on the net before they left for the airport.

Grandma stepped into her room with a guilty look on her face.

"How you feeling, baby?"

Amber shrugged. "Confused."

"I know you have a lot of questions. It'll give us a lot to talk about on the flight. Are you ready to go?"

Amber sat on her bed. "I don't know."

Grandma sat beside Amber. "You can still change your mind."

"No, I can't," Amber replied. "How do you say no when you're told the fate of the world is in your hands?"

"That's a good point," Grandma admitted. "For what it's worth this will be easy."

"Have you done it before, Grandma?"

"Done what?"

"Picked a Sana."

Grandma looked away. "No. But I was trained to and I'll be with you all the way."

"Great," Amber said as she frowned. "We both won't know what we're doing."

"Shush, child," Grandma scolded. "My father will make sure all goes well."

The doorbell rang and Amber answered. Javan entered with a wide smile on his handsome sepia face.

"Bon jour, ladies! Ready for your trip to the City of Lights?"

Amber looked at her grandmother and Javan. "You knew?"

Amber didn't think Javan's grin could get wider, but it did.

"Of course I knew. You'll love it!"

He took their bags to the jeep and they set off for the airport. He took the highway instead of the back roads, arriving at the airport in thirty minutes. He parked at the departure curb then took out their bags.

"I'll keep an eye on the bungalow Miss Corliss," Javan said.

"Thank you, Javan."

"You have a great time, Amber." He leaned over and kissed her on the cheek then kissed Grandma on the cheek as well. "Be good, the both of you."

Javan waved as he walked away.

"Such a sweet boy," Grandma commented.

Amber said nothing. She stared at Javan as he walked away, her hand resting on the cheek Javan had just kissed.

"Stop mooning and come on, girl." Grandma tugged Amber's arm. "Such behavior is unbecoming of a Seer."

Amber walked backwards waving at Javan until he sped away. She turned to Grandma who shook her head.

"Boy crazy, just like your mother," Grandma commented. "It took me everything in my power to keep that girl from getting pregnant before she was married."

"Grandma!' Amber exclaimed. "That's way too much information!"

"You're on your way to be a Seer, Amber. We must speak as equals now."

"Well, since we're equals and all, I think I need to call Mama and Daddy and let them know where we're going."

Grandma's eyes bulged. "We can't!"

"I don't mean tell them we're going to Marai. I know they won't believe that. I'm still not sure I do. But I have to tell them we're going to Paris. They should at least know that much."

Grandma nodded. "That's true. Let's get checked in then we'll call them."

The check in went smoothly. They boarded the small jet then hopped to Atlanta. They had an hour layover before their connecting flight to Paris. Amber gave Grandma her cell phone and she dialed Amber's parents.

"Hi baby!" Mama sang. "I wondered when you were going to call us."

"Crystal, it's Mama."

"Mama? Hi Mama. How are you doing? How's Amber?"

"She's fine. Look Crystal, Amber and I are taking a little trip. We'll be gone a couple of weeks."

"A trip? Where? You didn't say anything about a trip."

"I know baby. This was kind of last minute."

"But still Mama, Amber is down there to spend some time with you. I don't think she was expecting to go somewhere else."

"Amber's fine, Crystal. She's excited about going."

Crystal was quiet for a moment. "Where are you going? Jacksonville? Charleston?"

Corliss cleared her throat. "Paris."

Crystal was quiet again. "Mama, I don't recall any towns near Hilton Head called Paris. Oh wait, there is Parris Island."

"I'm talking about Paris, France, baby."

"Sam! Sam!" Crystal screamed. "Mama, don't you hang up this phone. Don't you dare!"

Grandma rolled her eyes and Amber giggled. She listened to Mama's hysterical voice as she told Daddy. The next voice she heard was his.

"Hello Mama Corliss. What's this I hear about you taking Amber to Paris?"

"Well Sam, Ben and I planned this trip a long time ago, but he died before we could take it. Since Amber had such a long time to visit, I thought this would be a good time to take advantage of all that saved up money."

"Mama Corliss, I understand how much you love Amber and how much you love spoiling her. But this is serious. You should have discussed this with Crystal and me first. We might have agreed, but under the circumstances I'm afraid we'll have to say no."

"Son, I understand how you feel, but it's a little too late for that. Amber and I are at Hartsfield waiting for our connecting flight."

"You're what? Mama Corliss, do not get on that flight! I will personally reimburse you for your tickets."

"Sam, don't worry about a thing. We'll be just fine. We'll call you as soon as we land. You two enjoy the Vineyard. Tell your Mama and them I said hello."

Grandma hung up and cut off the phone before handing it back to Amber.

"Do not turn that phone back on until we're in Paris," she ordered.

Amber saluted. "Yes ma'am!"

They boarded their Air France flight to Paris. Grandma had purchased first class seats, Amber's second first class flight. They settled in side by side for the eight-hour flight. Amber won over the flight staff as always with her polite charm and Grandma added to the take over with her elderly grace.

"Get some sleep," Grandma advised. "We may have a long day tomorrow."

"Why didn't you tell grandpa about Marai?" Amber asked, totally ignoring Grandma's' advice.

"You know how your grandfather was," Grandma answered. "Do you think he would have believed me?"

"I guess not. But he was your husband. You're not supposed to have any secrets from him."

Grandma laughed. "You're showing your age, baby girl. By the time I met your grandfather I didn't want to say anything about Marai."

"Why not?"

Grandma looked solemn. "I thought I made a big mistake by leaving. It took me a long time to get used to this world and when I did I didn't like what I saw. I couldn't understand why people hated each other just because of the color of their skin. I often thought about going back. But then I met your grandfather and fell in love."

Amber looked skeptical. "Grandpa didn't seem like a romantic type."

"He was old when you met him," Grandma said with a smile. "When I met him, he was an eighteen-year-old bricklayer with arms like the branches of a live oak and a smile that made me dizzy. The first time he kissed me I thought I was going to melt."

"Eeww!" Amber exclaimed.

"I know you've kissed a boy by now."

Amber sipped on her orange juice. "I don't have a problem with kissing. I have a problem about you and grandpa kissing."

"We did a lot more than that."

"Please, Grandma."

Grandma laughed. "Get some sleep, girl. This is an eight-hour flight."

Amber thought she would be too excited to sleep but she was wrong. When she awoke they were on the final approach to Charles De Gaulle airport, the sun hidden behind a rank of grey clouds.

"Bonjour!" the attendant announced. "Welcome to The City of Lights."

Amber looked out her window to the airport below. Paris sparkled in the pre-dawn darkness, earning its nickname. She reached back and shook Grandma.

"Grandma, we're here!"

Grandma woke up and looked toward the window. "It seems we are."

They disembarked then made their way quickly through the terminal. Taxis waited outside like mechanical sentinels, whisking travelers away to their varied destinations. One particular taxi driver caught Grandma's attention, his dark skin in stark contrast to his bright yellow shirt. A leather jacket hung from his narrow shoulders, barely reaching the top of his skinny jeans.

"Grandma, are you checking that young man out?" Amber asked.

"Don't be silly, girl," Grandma replied. "He reminds me of someone from home."

"Javan?"

"No, my real home. Marai."

Bonjour, mademoiselles," he said with a distinctive accent. "Where can I take you?"

"*L'Hotel Bristol*," Grandma replied.

"*Et pouvez-vous dépêcher s'il vous plaît?*"

Amber didn't understand the taxi driver's reply for he answered in French. She stared at Grandma in wonder.

"You speak French?"

Grandma smiled. "A special talent of a Seer. You can, too. Try it."

Amber tapped the taxi driver on his shoulder. "Excuse me, but how far will we be from the Louvre?"

"Not far," he replied. "I hope you get a chance to see all the sites. Paris is a beautiful city."

Amber was stunned. Though her ears heard the man's respond in French, the words registered in English in her mind. Her words apparently were spoken in French for the driver responded without hesitation.

"Cool! I'm taking French next year!" she exclaimed.

"Get in the car, baby girl," Grandma said with a smile.

Amber was captivated by the ride to the hotel. They drove through the roundabout encircling the Arc de Triumph. In the distance she could see the Eiffel Tower. She nearly fainted when she saw the hotel, an elegant building built in a 19th century style. The front entrance glittered with lights like Christmas.

"Grandma! This is beautiful! How can you afford this?"

"Your grandfather and I save up a long time for this trip," she replied. "We didn't plan on spending this much for a room but you and I won't be staying long. I decided we needed to pamper ourselves before we set out for Marai."

They checked in and went immediately to their suite. The huge room was filled with antique furniture and dazzling paintings. An enormous king size bed filled the bedroom.

"I hope you don't mind sleeping with an old lady," Grandma said.

"Not in this bed!" Amber fell backwards into the lush comforter and closed her eyes, a blissful smile on her face.

* * *

Corliss shook her head as she ambled into the bathroom. As she closed the door behind her a serious expression ruled her face. She reached into her purse, extracting a small leather pouch. She opened it and poured its contents into her hand. The grey dust she held was old, older than her, probably older that Marai. She raised her hand to her mouth, prepared to blow the powder onto the mirror. The dust would transform the glass to a portal where she could communicate with her father. She would tell him their location and he would send someone to meet them. Corliss pursed her lips then stopped. There was still time, she reasoned. Two days was not a long time, especially in the life of a Maraibu. For Amber, it could be two wonderful days in one of the most beautiful cities in the world before the weight of responsibility came crashing down. She put the powder back into the pouch and placed it back in her purse. Marai could wait a little longer.

CHAPTER FOURTEEN

Bissau stepped out of his hotel into the gray Parisian morning. He wrapped his arms around himself, shivered and cursed. He hated Paris. It was too wet, too rude and too foreign. He'd been waiting for days, looking into his mirror anxiously for word that Alake and Amber had arrived. He flagged a taxi and began a daily ritual, paying for the long ride to a neighborhood on the south side of the city, a neighborhood filled with people from home. They spoke Bambara differently than he, if they spoke it at all, so he was reduced to using the annoying language of the natives of the city. It seemed awkward speaking to faces so familiar in a language so strange, but that was the world outside. The food was familiar; the savory flavors brought images of Marai's swaying towers to his weary mind. His experiences among these outside folks made him more determined to insure the Veil remained between his city and this vileness.

He headed back to the hotel after a hearty breakfast. His room was comfortable yet modest based on what was available. Bissau tried to occupy himself by watching the television but he was disgusted by most of what he witnessed on the black screen. It took him a while to determine that every image coming across the device was not real; some images were based on actual happenings while others were like the plays held in the market during week's end. If what he saw was a reflection of this world, it gave him more reasons to reject it. Sometimes he wondered if Bagule had the right idea. This world was in need of a cleansing and Jakada was much too benevolent to administer such a punishment. He shook the thought out of his head. Bagule's evil might be what this world deserved, but it would swallow Marai as well. That he could not allow.

Bissau jumped from his seat and went to his bedroom mirror. The seeing dust rested atop the dresser and he picked it up, checking the contents. He was running low; he needed to save as much as possible for their return. He knew Alake possessed a portion but her supply was old and might have lost some of its potency over the years. Against his better judgment he removed a pinch and blew it into the mirror. The glass wavered, rippling like a disturbance in a bucket of water. Images appeared, faces of Parisians skimming across the reflective surface too fast for normal eyes but just the right speed for Bissau. He chanted as he scanned the images, hoping to find something among the throng to let him know Alake and Amber had arrived.

"You're wasting your time," Jakada said.

The images dissipated, replaced by the angry countenance of his mentor. Bissau dropped to his knees, his head lowered.

"Forgive me, Jele. I embarrass myself."

"Yes, you do," Jakada scolded. "I choose you for your reason and maturity. Don't make me regret my decision."

"I'm sorry, Jele."

Jakada nodded. "Your impatience is not why I contacted you. Bagule has discovered our plans."

Bissau jumped up. "How?"

"Traitors in my household," Jakada said, the disbelief apparent in his voice.

"Who?" Bissau asked.

Jakada's face took on a pained look.

"Hindolo."

"The cook?"

Jakada nodded. "I would not have known if I had not sensed the gris-gris added to my yams. I summoned him to my chamber then confronted him. Apparently his family owes a great debt to Bagule and this was his way of paying it back. He was afraid what I might do to him, so he shared Bagule's plans with me."

Bissau didn't like the sound of Jakada's voice.

"What has he done?"

"Bagule sent Aisha to stop Alake and Amber."

"The shape shifter?"

"Yes. Since she is not Maraibu she can pass through the Veil." Jakada stepped closer to his mirror. "You must go to them as soon as they contact you. I don't know if Aisha knows you are in Paris. That is your advantage. Do not fail me, Bissau."

Bissau's back straightened, the new urgency pushing away his anxiousness.

"I won't, Jele. I will bring them home, even if I have to kill Aisha to do it."

CHAPTER FIFTEEN

Aisha knew she would have to change her wardrobe the moment she stepped off the plane in Paris. The reason was practical as much as it was vain; the wardrobe she selected in Senegal was beautiful there but drew attention in Paris. Besides, she needed a variety of outfits to match whatever form she had to take in order to perform her task.

The wonders of the changed world still amazed her but she found herself less impressed the more she was exposed. The purpose of her journey took precedent over any personal excitement. A sensation permeated her joy, an indication that whomever she sought was close. Aisha hurried to the nearest taxi, her destination the Park Hyatt Paris. A passenger on the plane told her about it, a place close enough to the sites of the city but secluded enough for privacy. She converted half of her gold to Euros while at the airport, stashing the remainder on her person and in a locker at the airport. Once she settled into her room she was off again, striding into the hotel lobby like a woman on a mission. The concierge met her at the door.

"Can I help you, mademoiselle?" he asked.

"I need to buy clothing," she said.

"I can call you a taxi," the concierge replied. "Where do you wish to shop?"

"I need your finest clothes. The market closest to the king's palace would be preferable."

The concierge smirked, annoying Aisha. She must have made some kind of error that amused him. She thought about beating him unconscious but she had more important things to do. The young man waved over a taxi.

"Take mademoiselle to Lafayette Maison," he said.

The taxi driver sped her to a city district that overwhelmed her. The market was almost as big as the entire city of Marai. The taxi driver opened her door and Aisha absently placed a handful of Euros in his palm.

"Mademoiselle! This is too much!'

"You deserve it. Wait for me, will you?"

The man tipped his hat. "Of course!"

Lafayette Maison was only the beginning. Aisha shopped the entire day at some of the finest establishments in Paris, building an extensive wardrobe for a man and woman. Though she hated shifting into male form, it might prove necessary to carry out her plan. Bagule's directions were simple and direct. She was to keep Alake and her granddaughter in Paris until the elders convened to select a new Sana. No harm was to come to either one unless absolutely necessary. Aisha was relieved with the last command. She would kill if she had to, but she preferred not to. Blood lingered on her heart too long, bringing nightmares and hours of pouring libations to the slain person's soul for forgiveness. She had no doubt of fulfilling her duty; Bagule would be the most powerful man in Marai once selected as Sana. With Jele Jakada forced to serve him, Bagule would be the most powerful man in the world.

Back at her room, Aisha settled into the business of finding Alake. She asked for a hotel room with a fireplace; only the most exclusive hotels in the city provided such an amenity. The Prestige Suite in the Park Hyatt Paris was such a room. Aisha tipped the bellboy generously and then locked the door quickly. She sighed; this was opulence beyond that of the Daal, an extravagance unimagined in Marai. She shook the thoughts from her head. It was the wealth of Marai that made such extravagance affordable. She dumped her packages on the bed and went to the fire, taking out a small pouch from her brand new Dolce purse. Aisha whispered the words taught to her by the jele as she opened the pouch and sprinkled the contents into the fire. A thick white smoke rose before her, forming a dense cloud obscuring the dancing flames. She placed the bag down beside her and blew into the smoke. It parted, revealing an image she did not expect. Instead of the location of Alake and her granddaughter she gazed upon the handsome serious face of a young Maraibu man. A lecherous smile came to her face.

"Ahh, Bissau," she said. "The right man at the wrong time. Jele Jakada sent you, no doubt." Her smile grew wider. This would be easy. She had imagined his face many times like most young women of the city. She watched him pace, noting his gestures and manners although she was familiar with his every move. Alake would know nothing about him other than his appearance; Jakada would be more difficult to fool. But Jakada was not here. She waved her hand and the view expanded, pulling away from Bissau's visage to the hotel in which he stayed. She memorized the name, saying it aloud in her best imitation of Bissau's baritone. It was then she began to transform, the muscles under her skin resembling playful children under a sepia blanket as they rearranged to match her latest disguise. Her breasts flattened and expanded, her shoulders rising and thickening. Facial features melded as her hair shortened. There was some pain, but not much. She stripped off her clothes and dressed in the men's garments she'd purchased earlier and then stood before the mirror, satisfied with the transformation.

"Now Bissau, it's time you met your better half," she said with a grin.

CHAPTER SIXTEEN

Jakada strolled down the narrow streets of Marai's main market-place trying to keep a worried frown from marring his usually stoic countenance. The sun lurked low overhead, its searing heat abating as it descended below Maria's walls. The market was lively as always; women in bright blue dresses and head wraps waved chickens at passersby while a solemn man in yellow and red sang patrons to his cart filled with woven baskets. Up ahead merchants and patrons yelled, argued and laughed as they haggled for their daily needs. This was the Sana's market, the market closest to the palace hence the reason for its activity. The provisions needed to provide for the royal family accounted for the bulk of the transactions. Maraibu traveled from the other city districts for the exotic items found only at the Sana market.

The merchants' voices grew louder, a sure sign of the presence of a wealthy patron. A line of broad muscular men emerged from the throng, their bodies bare to the waist, their legs covered by white pants gathered about their waists with purple sashes. Each man held a thick staff which they used to clear the way, pushing back the overzealous sellers. Jakada's sour mood broke through his façade when he recognized who the bodyguards served. The men displayed serpent bracelets coiled around their thick forearms, Bagule's family talisman. He could barely see the top the elder's purple turban over the wall of guards. The men approached him and broke their line, allowing him inside. Bagule stood before him pulling at his narrow beard, Nieleni at his side. Both were richly dressed as befitting a couple of high lineage. The men bowed, shook hands and kissed each other's cheek.

"A good day for a walk I see," Bagule said. "It is a rare day Marai's Jele is seen among the common folk."

"It seems the day brought us both out of hiding," Jakada answered. "I hope all is well."

"Any better and I would think the ancestors were ready to call me home," Bagule replied.

Jakada looked at Nieleni and she looked away with a smile. A purple and white headscarf covered her braids; huge crescent gold earrings dangled beside her charming face. A single golden hoop accented with a small diamond pierced her nose and an amber necklace encircled her graceful neck. He wondered how a woman so striking would agree to marry Bagule. The union was a definite step up for her family but Jakada refused to think of the consequences. She seemed happy enough on the outside, but one never knew what secrets hid behind the eyes.

"You seem distracted my friend," Bagule said. "Are you sure all is well?"

"The Sana's condition is a constant concern," Jakada confessed. "I would feel better if there was something I could do."

"Death comes for us all," Bagule said. "It is the one reality in which we all are equal."

The merchants were getting belligerent, their loud pleas making it difficult for the two men to talk.

"I think I've had enough of this beautiful day," Jakada said. "Work waits. Be well, Bagule."

The two men bowed to each other and continued on their separate ways. Jakada glanced back and met Nieleni's smirking face. *You're being watched*, her expression conveyed. Their meeting in the market was not a coincidence. Jakada had purged his servants of any interlopers, but he could not prevent anyone watching from outside. He hurried back to his home and ran up the stairs to his mirror room. He sat for a moment to catch his breath then whispered the spell, bringing the reflective glass to life. He peered into Alake's room. The lights were dim; apparently they were asleep. He whispered his daughter's name but there was no response. His forehead throbbed; his daughter was ignoring him, determined to show her granddaughter a grand time in Paris before setting the weight of a kingdom on her shoulders. But there was no more time. Bagule's confidence was a bad sign. He had to get Amber to Marai before Bagule tried to force his hand. It never occurred to him until the market that Bagule might attempt to expedite the Sana's demise. Despite his foul mind Bagule was a man of tradition; tradition did not speak against assassination as long as the assassin was of royal lineage, which Bagule was. He was just as much a candidate for succession as were much more worthy men.

Jakada gave up on Alake and summoned Bissau. The young man staggered to the mirror rubbing his eyes.

"Yes, Jele?" he croaked.

"Bissau, I need you to find Alake and Amber immediately. Time is running out."

"I thought you wanted me to wait for them to contact me."

"I fear Bagule may attempt to rush things."

Bissau was suddenly alert. "How could he do so?"

Jakada sighed before answering. "He may try to kill the Sana."

"I still don't know where they are Jele," Bissau confessed. "Do you have the name of their hotel?"

Jakada scowled. "No. Alake has not told me. I must depend on you to find it."

"Paris is a big city with many hotels, Jele. It will be difficult."

"But it can be done," Jakada finished.

Bissau shoulders slumped. "I will try, Jele."

"Remember why I chose you, Bissau. This is your duty, not some willful challenge. We must get Alake and Amber to Marai before the Sana's passing!"

"Yes, Jele," Bissau rubbed his eyes. "I will find them. I will start looking now."

"Good. Contact me when you have found them. I will try to prepare a portal for you nearby."

"Yes, Jele." Bissau dropped his head, despair on his face as his visage faded.

Jakada sat on his stool in despair. He made a mistake sending Bissau. He thought the young man's combination of skill and resilience would help him shoulder the strangeness of the outside world while carrying out his task. Apparently he was wrong. Bissau's eyes told him that the boy was overcoming the man, and the boy wanted to come home with or without Alake and Amber. He would have to contact him daily to build his spirits, a taxing endeavor but necessary. He would not let Bagule win.

CHAPTER SEVENTEEN

The Eiffel Tower shone against the Parisian night sky, attended by a bright full moon. Amber and Grandma strolled down the street, their arms joined like old friends. This was the best summer vacation ever, at least so far. Her pending duty loomed before her but she did her best to block it out. There was a saying to live for the moment and Amber was doing exactly that.

"There is something I must tell you," Grandma said, breaking her momentary bliss. "Tomorrow I will tell my father where we are. Before I do, I must teach you how to use the amber necklace."

Amber let go of Grandma's arm and stepped back, almost running into the young couple sauntering behind them.

"Pardon moi," she said. The couple weaved around them, smiling as they walked away.

"Read them," Grandma said.

"I don't feel like it," Amber replied.

"When you stand before the Elders of Marai to choose the new Sana, how you feel won't matter. It will be the most important decision of your life and the people of my city. There will be no room for selfish feelings."

Amber had never seen her Grandma so serious. She searched the elder woman's eyes for a bit of sympathy but found none. She concentrated on the man first.

"He's in love with her. He has been for a long time. Their relationship is new and he's thinking marriage one day."

"Now her," Grandma ordered.

"She's not as happy. She just broke up with a man she loved deeply. This man is a distraction until she heals. She doesn't see a future with him. She thinks he's weak for loving her so much."

Grandma smiled as she came to stand beside her. "Now, grasp the necklace and read both of them again."

Amber grasped the necklace and was jolted by a bright flash. There was darkness; she groped for Grandma and felt a tight squeeze of her hand.

"I'm right here, baby," Grandma said.

Amber squeezed Grandma's hand for assurance then searched the darkness for the couple. Colors walked before her, hues in human form travelling the streets of Paris. She found the couple and though she couldn't distinguish their features she knew it was them. The man pulsed with a fuchsia hue; the woman radiated dark blue.

"The man is joy, she whispered, "the woman is pain."

"You see their feelings," Grandma replied. "Now you must see their ka."

"Ka?" Amber tried to remove her hand from the necklace but Grandma stopped her with a quick hand squeeze.

"The ka is the soul. It is the truth of what we are. To see the ka is to know what a person is. Concentrate, Amber!"

Amber felt her eyes clench as she focused on the couple. The competing colors faded away, replaced by a faint green glow.

"They are good." The words sprang from her lips before she had time to think. "They will fall in love and marry."

Grandma took her hand from the necklace. There was another bright flash and the world was normal again.

"That is your gift, Amber. You have the power to see the essence of a man or woman, to know how they will live their lives. With your gift you will select Marai's next Sana."

Amber's stomach tightened. "What if I'm wrong?

"You can't be." Grandma patted her hand. "This ability is natural to you. It's like breathing. You cannot control what you see, nor can a person hide their ka from you. You will always know their true self."

Amber's legs weakened. She found a bench and sat. "That explains so much."

Grandma sat beside her. "What are you talking about?"

Amber looked into Grandma's loving eyes. She always truly listened to her. Mama and Daddy tried, but they were too anxious to give advice to really hear what she had to say. Grandma had the patience of the ages and now she knew why. Still, it was hard for her to speak.

"I don't have many friends, Grandma," Amber began. "Most kids don't like me because they say I'm mean. I say things that hurt their feelings. The really bad part is that I'm usually right."

"I would suspect you're always right, even if they don't admit it."

Amber shrugged. "Grownups don't care too much for me either. I manage not to be rude most of the time, but sometimes it just slips out. Now I know why."

"It was the same for me, Amber." Grandma patted her hand. "That's why I ran away. I wanted to be normal and I knew I couldn't be as long as I remained in Marai."

"How old were you when you left?"

Grandma smiled. "Thirteen."

Amber's eyes reflected her shock. "You came all the way from Africa to America when you were thirteen?"

"I had some help," Grandma answered. "My father taught me a few spells that helped me survive the desert. They also helped me hide on a ship headed to America. The skills faded as I became older. By the time I met your grandfather my nyama had faded completely. I was normal and I loved it."

Amber was confused. "Nyama?"

"You call it magic, but that's not the right term," Grandma replied. "It's all that and more."

"You lost the sight?"

"No, child, I didn't lose the sight. I found your grandfather with my gift. His soul was golden, but I didn't need to see inside him to know. I lost the nyama my father taught me, not that which was natural to me. But it didn't matter. I never planned on going back."

"And now you must," Amber said.

Grandma patted her hand. "We'll be fine. Baba is sending someone to escort us home. I'm sure whoever he chooses will be more than capable for the task."

Grandma stood. "Come on now. It's time for bed. It's way past my curfew."

Amber grasped Grandma's hand. They were more alike than her and Mama. That's why Grandma gave her the necklace instead of Mama. She looked into the sky, memorizing the stars and the moon as she listened to the sounds around her that were different, yet familiar. After tomorrow, the world would never be the same.

CHAPTER EIGHTEEN

The urgent knocking on his door snatched Bissau from a dreamless sleep. His head jerked up; his eyes were wide and blinking although he still could not see. He rubbed them with his fists and vision returned. The features of his room took shape in the dim light of his computer monitor. For a moment he couldn't remember why he sat before the foul contraption until the image of the hotel filling the screen jarred his thoughts. He had found where Alake and her granddaughter were staying, but he was so tired after he found it he fell asleep at the desk.

The door thumped again.

"Coming!" he shouted. He trudged to the door and opened it without peering through the peephole.

"Yes?" he said. The hallway light blurred his view.

"Perfect," the voice replied.

"What are you ...by the ancestors!"

Bissau was looking at himself. The other Bissau was dressed more like the French, but the face was an exact copy of his. Before he could speak the other Bissau shoved him back into the room and slammed the door.

"I don't want to hurt you," the doppelganger said. "You're too handsome to harm." He opened his hand and revealed a white pouch.

"Take this," he said.

Danger cleared Bissau's mind. He slapped the mysterious twin's hand away and kicked him in the chest, knocking him across the room and into the door. His twin looked stunned for a minute then leered at him.

"You're quick, too," He approached Bissau like a lion moving on a rival cat. "Too bad it has to be this way. I might have to damage that pretty face."

The doppelganger lunged at Bissau. The young warrior immediately snapped a kick but his opponent was gone. Bissau's supporting leg was swept from under him and he crashed onto the floor. He rolled away before the knee meant for his chest came down, pushing up with his hands and crouching low. His second attack was more successful; his fist grazed his attacker's face, knocking him against the bed. He leapt at the interloper and was engulfed by a cloud of white dust. Feeling left his body and he crashed face first into the floor.

He couldn't feel the hands that turned him onto his back. The mirror image of his face looked at him with true regret.

"You'll be fine," he said. "But I think your nose is broken. I'm sorry."

The face vibrated and twisted; suddenly Bissau was looking upon a woman's face, a countenance from his home. It was Aisha, the shape shifter. She leaned close to him and kissed him on the cheek.

"Such a beautiful boy," she whispered. "Maybe Bagule will let me have you once Marai is his."

Her face contorted back to his form. He watched her saunter to the computer.

"Excellent!" she exclaimed. "This is exactly what I was searching for. Thank you, Bissau. Rest well. Once this is done I will come back for you. This will be my city, and you will be mine, too."

She kissed him one more time and left him paralyzed on the floor. He made a promise as she closed the door. The next time he saw Aisha, he would kill her.

CHAPTER NINETEEN

Amber couldn't sleep. She leaned against her window sill, staring out into the Parisian night. She was learning so much about herself, answering quiet questions that had rustled in her mind since she could remember. The sudden visions that laid a person's emotions bare to her made sense now. For so long she thought she was a mean person; now she knew she was expressing a talent she couldn't control. It didn't take away the pain, but knowing made it easier to deal with.

Her musing was interrupted by a tapping on the hotel door. She tensed; who would be knocking at this time of night?

"Don't answer it, baby," her grandmother said. She rose up from the bed, concern on her face. "I'll call the desk."

"Mama Alake?" The voice seeped under the door and Amber jumped. Her grandmother scrambled from the bed and donned her house robe. She shuffled to the door.

"Who is it?" she challenged.

"It is I, Bissau," the voice answered back. "I have come for you and your granddaughter."

Grandma's eyes widened and a smile came to her face, a smile so joyous Amber smiled as well.

"We are close now, Amber!" She opened the door wide and Amber's smile faded. Bissau, the man sent to escort them to Marai, was a boy. Not necessarily a boy, for he was at least Amber's age. He was definitely not what she expected, but he was handsome, very handsome. There was something else as well, a feeling that seemed to shout for attention but she couldn't grasp. She was too busy staring at him.

Bissau looked at them and returned their generous smiles. "It is an honor to meet both of you, but time is short. I apologize for my delay. There are others that do not wish to see you return to Marai."

Grandma's face became concerned. "I understand. We will pack immediately. Come, Amber. We must hurry."

Amber lingered as she stared, trying to decipher the feeling of doubt flittering in her mind. Bissau's smile disappeared to a look of nervous concern.

"Honored lady, do you feel well?" he asked.

"I'm fine," she replied. She backed away and followed her Grandma to her room.

"Grandma, are you sure about this?"

Grandma looked into Amber's eyes. "I know it seems strange to you that such a young man would be sent to us, but in Marai Bissau is a man. He has done things that boys his age in this world couldn't imagine, and if my father sent him he must be a young man of many talents."

Amber couldn't shake her doubt despite Grandma's words. "You know this world more than I, but something doesn't seem right."

"This is new to you and your talents are still raw. Trust me, Amber. Now go pack your things."

Amber went to her room, glancing at Bissau as she entered. He looked at her and smiled. Her cheeks warmed and she turned away. She packed her luggage, scouring the room one more time to make sure she didn't forget anything. Once everything was packed she looked into the mirror to make sure her hair was straight. She also wished she had some makeup, but neither Mama nor Grandma would stand for that. She sighed then left the room. When she came into the sitting area Grandma and Bissau waited. They were about to leave the room when Grandma held up her hand.

"Wait, I must let baba know you have come," she said.

"We have no time," Bissau said sternly. "The taxi is waiting downstairs and our flight leaves soon."

"Flight?" Grandma looked puzzled and Amber's worry escalated. "I thought we were going to use a mirror."

Bissau looked confused for a moment before replying. "Powers reach out from the city, disrupting the Jele's plans. We must use what works."

Amber looked into her Grandma's face and saw worry. Her Grandma gazed back and grasped her hand. She was trembling.

"I was hoping we would return to Marai unnoticed but that is not to be," she said. "We must be careful now. If someone attempts to harm us beyond the Veil it means they have defied that which was decreed long ago. Stay close to me, Amber."

Amber squeezed her Grandma's hand. "I will, Grandma."

"Come, we must leave now," Bissau urged.

They followed their guardian to the elevator and into the lobby. Grandma checked out and they exited into the night and into the taxi. The three sat together in the back seat, Grandma sitting between Amber and Bissau. Amber let out a sigh. She was hoping to sit beside him.

Bissau leaned forward to look at them both, his eyes lingering on Amber.

"Our flight will take us to Dakar. From there we'll link up with Tuaregs and travel into the desert to their salt camp. I'll lead us to Marai."

The taxi stopped before the gates and they entered the airport. Bissau went to the ticket counter and purchased their tickets. He came back to them with a childish smile on his face.

"Have you ever flown before, Amber?"

Amber looked confused. "How do you think we got here?"

Bissau laughed. "Yes, yes, of course. I apologize. This is all new to me. But don't worry. Once we get to the desert I will be in complete control."

Amber looked at her Grandma. Grandma looked back with an amused grin.

"You'll have plenty of stories to tell when we return to Marai."

"Yes indeed." Bissau handed them their tickets. "I got us first class seats. They're much more comfortable." He raised his hand before Amber could scold him.

"You know this, of course."

"Of course," Amber snapped. Despite his good looks Bissau was beginning to get on her nerves.

*   *   *

The real Bissau strained to move his legs, then his arms, then finally his head. Nothing cooperated. Aisha's paralyzing powder had kept him immobile for hours, locked in an awkward pose. The sun crept through the blinds, slipping across the carpeted floor to rest across his eyes.

"Monsieur? Monsieur?"

Bissau watched the door knob twist and the door ease open. The maid stuck her head in and looked around.

"Bonjour, monsieur!" She opened the door wide and rolled in her cart. She was heading to the bathroom when she saw him sprawled on the floor, looking up at her with glazed eyes. She screamed and ran from the room.

Bissau struggled to move and was rewarded with sensation in his left foot. He was working his ankle when the paramedics arrived. They crouched around him, speaking French too fast for him to understand. A stretcher was rolled into the room then the paramedics lifted him onto it. Ceiling lights streaked past his eyes as he trundled to the elevator then down to the lobby and into the ambulance. Feeling progressed up his foot to his leg and his right foot was beginning to move as well but he remained still. There was no reason to do anything now. If he moved or spoke they would ask questions he could not answer. So he remained silent as sensation crept throughout his body. The ambulance careened through traffic, the high speed just as disconcerting as Aisha's powder. It pulled into the emergency entrance and Bissau was rolled into the hospital, surrounded by babbling Frenchmen. He was taken to a private room, undressed him then wrapped him in a robe-like shirt that tied in the back. His arm was pricked and he was hooked to a bag of water. The nurse, a black woman who spoke French as if it was her homeland, tried to soothe his nerves.

"You'll be alright, *mon ami*," she assured him. "This is the best hospital in Paris. We'll find out what's wrong with you."

"Where are my clothes?" he asked.

The nurse pointed at a bag resting in a metal chair.

"Don't worry. The doctor will be here shortly."

No sooner did the nurse leave did Bissau jump up from the bed then carefully remove the needle from his arm. He stumbled to his clothes thensearched his pockets and found a small amount of mirror dust. He wasn't sure if it was enough to contact Jakada but he had to try. He shuffled to the small mirror hanging over the sink and blew the dust into the mirror. The glass shimmered and his reflection disappeared. After a few moments Jakada's face appeared.

"Bissau, do you have Alake and Amber?" Jakada asked.

Bissau dropped his head, embarrassed. "No, Jele. Aisha attacked me in my room. She has assumed my identity. I fear that Alake and Amber are with her."

Jakada closed his eyes then opened them, his expression serious.

"Put your hands on the mirror," he ordered.

Bissau put his hands on the glass. Jakada placed his hands opposite Bissau's and a blinding jolt consumed Bissau. His mind cleared and the dregs of Aisha's concoction dissipated. Jakada dropped his hands and released his protégé.

Jakada's image wavered. "I have passed you my nyama. It will take time for me to recover. Until then you are on your own. Find my daughters. Stop Aisha."

Jakada disappeared. Bissau felt renewed, although guilt and disappointment accompanied his new energy. Jakada felt him not capable of aiding his daughters on his own so he had sacrificed his own nyama to help him.

"I will not fail you, Jele," he whispered.

Bissau dressed quickly. He was zipping his pants when the nurse's voice interrupted him.

"Mr. Bissau!"

Bissau spun to see the nurse and a man he assumed was the doctor staring at him. The man wore a white coat with some type of instrument hanging from his neck. He reminded Bissau of a Marai healer.

"Hello, I'm Dr. Dubois," the tall bearded man said.

"Thank you for your help, but I am fine," Bissau said. He attempted to leave but the doctor grabbed his arm.

"You can't leave just yet. You were paralyzed. Although I'm glad to see you standing you must stay. We don't know what caused your paralysis and it might happen again."

Bissau's eyes narrowed. "I know what caused it and it will not happen again, not if I can help it."

The doctor tightened his grip. "Monsieur, please."

Bissau shrugged and the doctor flew from his feet and into the wall. Bissau stared at the unconscious man, stunned by his new-found strength. The nurse stumbled away, her hands flying over her mouth.

Bissau ran from the room as the nurse screamed. He slid across the floor then winced as he slammed against the wall. He steadied then ran to the end of the hall to the exit stairs. He burst outside into the crowded street, startled Parisians staring and pointing at him as he continued running. He didn't stop until he was blocks away, amazed with his new-found talents. He was barely winded though he had run miles. But Bissau had no illusions about his powers. They were temporary. He didn't know how long they would last but he would use his time wisely. He would find Alake and Amber.

CHAPTER TWENTY

Amber stared out the window as the Air France flight cruised over the shores of Senegal. Grandma sat beside her fast asleep. How could she? Amber thought. They were running from who knows what to who knows where and Grandma snored beside her as if they were taking a trip to Disney World. She leaned forward to look to the opposite row. Bissau's face was pressed against the window. He turned suddenly to look at her as if he expected to see her, his eyes sparkling in perfect harmony with his glittering teeth.

"You should see this!" he said. "It's amazing. Everything looks so small!"

She smiled back at him nervously then sat back in her seat.

"Okay girl, get a hold of yourself," she whispered. It didn't matter that Bissau was cute. She was in the middle of an adventure she couldn't have dreamed up if she wanted. This couldn't be real, yet it was. She closed her eyes and tried to imagine things different but she couldn't. She was on her way to Senegal to save a kingdom. This was crazy.

The captain announced their approach. Amber placed her hand on Grandma's shoulder then shook her easy.

"Grandma, we're landing. You got to sit up and buckle your seatbelt."

Grandma turned toward her and her eyes cracked open.

"What you say, baby?"

"We're landing, Grandma. Put on your seatbelt."

"Landing? What are you…oh! We're landing in Senegal!"

Grandma sat straight and leaned past Amber to peer out the window.

"I'm home, Amber!" she sang. "I'm home."

Amber looked into Grandma's eyes as she sat back in her seat. There was a gleam in her eyes, a light she hadn't noticed since grandpa died. Her face seemed brighter, almost younger as she snapped her seat belt and snuggled into the seat.

"I didn't think I would be this excited," Grandma admitted.

"How long has it been?"

"A very long time, baby."

She glanced at Bissau. His face was still pinned to the window.

"I'm not sure about him," Amber said.

"Don't worry." Grandma looked his way and then back at Amber. "This is all new to him. The Outside is probably a wonderful place for him. It was for me."

"He's acting so childish!"

"Once we land he will be in control, I'm sure. It's the part of the journey that he is more than familiar with," Grandma assured her.

The plane jerked as the landing gear touched the tarmac. It cruised for a few minutes then halted near the terminal. Amber watched the stair car approaching and her stomach tightened.

"Okay, here we go!" she whispered.

Bissau led them down the stairs. Amber followed, hesitating at the bottom. She looked about then placed her foot on African soil. Her head spun as a bright flash blinded her. She stumbled and someone grabbed her before she fell to the ground. She opened her eyes to a smiling female face.

"Thank you," she said.

"You're welcome." The woman kept grinning as she helped Amber steady.

Grandma came to her side. "Father chose a good man, just like I said. Thank you, Bissau."

Amber froze. She looked at Grandma then back at the woman helping her stand. She looked around her. Bissau was nowhere to be seen. But this woman…

"I can help you to the terminal, Amber. We'll get our bags and be on our way."

Amber stared into the woman's eyes. This was not Bissau holding her. This was a woman, but she talked as if she was Bissau. A chill shot up her back and she clinched her teeth. Her mind worked in slow motion toward a conclusion that she didn't believe even though the truth stood before her smiling.

"Grandma, can you help me?"

"Of course, baby. Bissau, you go ahead and get our bags."

The woman smiled and trotted away. As soon as Grandma reached her Amber grabbed her tight.

"That's not Bissau!" she shrieked.

Grandma's eyes widened. "What are you talking about?"

"It's not Bissau! It's a woman!"

"Slow down, baby girl. Tell me what's going on."

"When my foot touched the tarmac, I saw a bright light then got really dizzy. Then she caught me. That's not Bissau."

Grandma pulled her away from the passengers. They shuffled toward the terminal but not to baggage claim.

"You say that is not Bissau and that it is a woman?"

"Yes! She talks like a man but it's a woman. I can see her!"

Grandma frowned. "There was a woman in Marai who could change her shape. She was not Maraibu. Baba wondered how she came to the city but never bothered her because she caused no harm. Bagule probably hired her because she could pass through the Veil. If she took Bissau's identity she may have done harm to him."

"What do we do?"

"We'll stay in Dakar as long as we can," Grandma decided. "I'm sure the real Bissau will come, but we'll have to avoid this woman until he arrives."

"But what if he doesn't?"

"Then we will go on our own."

Amber's mouth became dry and her eyes widened. "We have no idea where to go."

"I'll admit my memory is not clear, but I know the way home."

Amber's eyes brightened. "I have an idea."

She grabbed Grandma's hand and together they ran for the airport entrance, pushing past the horde of men hawking baggage assistance. They went to the curb and Amber flagged down a taxi.

"Where to?" the driver asked in French.

"The American Embassy," Amber replied.

They climbed in and the driver sped away. Amber looked back to see the woman standing at the curb, staring at the taxi in with an angry look twisting her face. Amber fell back into her seat.

"She saw us, but it doesn't make a difference. We'll be safe in the embassy."

Grandma didn't look convinced.

"It always works in the movies," Amber said. "We're American citizens. We'll tell them we felt threatened and needed a safe place to rest for a minute."

"We won't be safe there, either," Grandma said. "She's a shape shifter. If she finds us she'll assume someone's identity to get inside."

"I'll know who she is."

"You will but the others won't. Do you think they'll believe you?"

Amber folded her arms across her chest and pouted. "If we go back home she'll leave us alone."

Grandma looked at her with concern. "Yes she would."

The taxi became silent. Amber understood Grandma's statement. They could go home and be safe. Whoever was after them would probably leave them alone. But what would happen to Marai?"

"We'll have to keep moving until we can find the real Bissau or make it to Marai on our own," she finally said. "We'll stay at the Embassy as long as we can then we'll …stay with boarders!"

"Boarders? We don't know anyone in Senegal."

"We can't go to any hotels," Amber explained. "It's the first place anyone would look. Maybe the Embassy has a list of families that take in tourists. I remember Daddy talking about his summer in Europe. He lived with local people so he could get the full taste of the culture. I think the Embassy may have some information on that. I hope they do."

"If we do this Bissau will have a hard time finding us, too."

"We can contact great grandfather and tell him what's happened. Maybe he can contact Bissau so we can tell him where we are."

The black and yellow taxi weaved through the narrow street of Dakar. Despite their dire situation Amber leaned against the window, taking in the sites as best she could. The streets were filled with black people rushing to and fro, some dressed casually like her friends in Atlanta while others wearing more traditional garb. The taxi driver meandered through the confusing streets but somehow, she was able to keep her sense of direction. She was changing with every moment that passed; her awareness increasing with each mile traveled.

The taxi finally parked before a large building surrounded by a brick fence. The American flag drooped on a flagpole within the walls; two Marines in battle fatigues flanked the gate.

Amber paid the driver. "Wait for us," she said.

The taxi driver nodded and lounged in his seat.

"Get your passport out, Grandma," Amber said.

"I see you're taking control of things quite well," Grandma commented.

"I'm sorry, Grandma. Am I being bossy?"

"No, baby. You're doing what you're supposed to do."

They showed their papers to the guards.

"The Consulate Receptionist can help you," one of the guards said.

They entered the building. The receptionist was a young woman with a short afro and a warm smile.

"Welcome to Senegal," she said. "How may I help you?"

Grandma ambled to the desk. "Hello. My grandbaby and I were wondering if there was a program for visitors to live with locals during their visit to Senegal."

The receptionist's face soured. "Ma'am, the proper procedure is to request a living visit prior to arriving."

Grandma smiled warmly. "I know, sweetheart, but this was an unexpected side trip. Could you at least check to see if anyone is available? This is her thirteenth birthday present and I want it to be special."

The woman's eyes brightened as she looked at Amber. "So you're a teenager now? Congratulations! Give me a minute; I'll see what I can do."

Amber calmed herself as the receptionist's manicured fingers raced across the keyboard. She stopped and grinned.

"Here's a family that might be interested," she said. "The Sonkos. Very friendly people. They own a nice house near the coast. I'll give them a call."

Grandma smiled then winked at Amber. "Thank you very much, daughter."

The woman nodded as she smiled at them.

"If it wasn't for the passports and the accents I would have taken you both for Senegalese," she commented.

Amber and Grandma stepped away from the desk while the receptionist called the Sonkos.

"Once we get with the Sonkos we can use their mirror to contact great grandfather," Amber whispered. "He can contact Bissau and tell him where we are."

"You don't think the imposter will find us?"

Amber's concern finally overtook her emotions. "I don't know what powers she possesses. I'm hoping she'll search the hotels first then maybe come here. She'll find us eventually. I'm praying that Bissau will find us first."

"Would you ladies like something to drink?" the receptionist called out.

"No thank you," Amber called back. She and Grandma sat on the bench near the embassy door and patiently waited for the Sonkos. She held Grandma's hand like she used to when they strolled the woods along the coast, winding through palmettos before reaching the hidden beaches trimmed with sea oats. If someone told her days ago that she would be sitting in Senegal fleeing a shape-shifter as she tried to find a hidden ancient kingdom to select its new king, she would have declared them insane. Grandma's hand was her anchor. As long as she was with her, everything happening was real.

A dusty black Mercedes rambled up to the embassy entrance, smoke belching from its tailpipe. A tall woman stepped out the passenger side, her dark skin in contrast to the brightly colored dress that hung slightly from her shoulder. A matching wrap adorned her head, a colorful collage that brought out her glowing smile. She swaggered to the embassy entrance.

"Bon jour!" She waved vigorously at the receptionist then aimed her enthusiasm at Amber and Grandma. Amber could see immediately that this woman was a kind soul. She didn't need her abilities to determine it.

"Hello, ladies! I am Madame Josephine. I hear you are looking for a place to stay as you experience our wonderful country."

Amber stood and took Madame Josephine's hand. "Bon jour, Madame. I'm Amber and this is my grandmother Corliss. You're beautiful."

"And you are so kind," Madame Josephine replied. "Come, come, we can talk on the way to my villa. I want to know all about you. And of course, I will tell you all about me!"

Madame Josephine waved goodbye to the receptionist and the trio hurried to her car. Josephine's chauffeur jumped from the driver's side and opened the doors for the ladies. Amber felt some relief; they would have time to relax while they figured out how to continue their journey. The cool air conditioning of the dated German sedan was comforting; Amber leaned back into the leather seats and closed her eyes. Despite the excitement of the Motherland she was exhausted. Apparently, fatigue was the consequence of her new abilities.

"Madame, you have a familiar face to me," Josephine said to Grandma.

"I doubt very seriously if you know me," Grandma replied.

Josephine broke into sparking laughter. "No, no I don't mean that kind of familiar. You look Senegalese. Something tells me your migration from home was very recent."

"Yes and no," Grandma replied. "It was and it wasn't."

Amber opened her eyes and grinned at Grandma. Josephine looked at them both with a puzzled expression.

"Really? You are a mystery I must solve. Excellent!"

They emerged from the crowded narrow streets to a wide boulevard that ran parallel to the ocean. Majestic villas lined the street opposite the shore. Miss Josephine smiled as they passed the row of lovely homes. The driver turned into a driveway bordered by sand colored walls topped with ceramic pots sprouting beautiful flowers. The ornate garage door before them lifted and the driver pulled inside.

"We're home!" Josephine announced. "Come, come!"

The driver opened their doors and they followed Josephine into her home.

"This is my palace," she said. "I'll take you to your rooms, and then I will show it to you."

Grandma looked at the steep staircase and took a deep breath.

"That's a long way up," she commented.

"Oh, do not worry, Madame," Josephine replied. "I have a wonderful room downstairs. I have so many and they are seldom used. Sometimes I ask myself why I have such a large house. Then I answer, because I can!"

Amber giggled then covered her mouth in embarrassment. She was too old for giggling. Josephine was such a bubbly woman it was hard not to be in a good mood around her. But the purpose of their visit loomed behind the good feelings. They had to get settled then get to a mirror so they could communicate with her great grandfather.

"I could really use a rest," Grandma said as he stared at Amber. "Come, come, I will show you your room."

Amber and Grandma followed Josephine down the hallway to the room. It was an opulent affair; the gaudy accoutrements anchored by a beautiful king size bed. The pillows and sheets were over the top for Dakar's climate but they made the statement that Madame Josephine was wealthy.

"It is a little thing, but I think you'll find it comfortable," Josephine said.

Grandma looked intimidated. "I think I will."

"Manifique!" Josephine exclaimed. "Now, little one, I will take you to your room. I'm sure you'll love it!"

Josephine strode from the room. Amber lingered for a moment.

"I'll be back soon," she whispered.

Grandma nodded. "We'll contact baba then."

"Amber?" Josephine called out.

Amber hurried to catch up to her patron. "I'm sorry, Madame. I had to make sure Grandma had her medicines."

A melancholy frown emerged on Josephine's face. "Ah, the ravages of age. It is sad we cannot avoid them. Time had been kind to me. I'm sure I am probably your mother's age and look at me. Sometimes I think time has stood still, but then I look at my grown children I realized I will soon be a grandmother. Me! A grandmother!"

She flipped her hand and her smile returned. "I'll worry about that when the time comes. Now follow me, I want you to see your room!"

Josephine glided up the staircase, Amber close behind. Amber had been polite so far, refusing to let her talents reveal more about Josephine. But the woman's last statement made her curious so she briefly let her ability tell her more about this gregarious woman. The emotion struck her deep, causing her hesitate on the stairs. Behind

Josephine's joyful exterior was extreme loneliness and sadness. There had been tragedy in her life, more than most people could handle and more than anyone deserved.

"Are you okay, dear?"

Josephine's worried expression told her that whatever she thought was apparently reflecting on her face.

"Yes Madame. I'm fine. Is this my room?"

Josephine's brightness returned. "Yes, it is!"

Amber stepped into a room she had only imagined in her dreams. Her parents were far from poor; if anything, they overindulged her. But this room was beyond anything they'd attempted and Amber knew why. It was a tribute to a child that had died too soon. Josephine apparently changed its setting to coincide with the child's age. By looks of it she would have been the same age as Amber.

"It's beautiful," Amber said.

Josephine hugged her. "I'm so glad you like it. It is the best room in the house."

Amber looked into Josephine's eyes. "I can tell in means a lot to you."

Madame Josephine's smile weakened. "It does, very much."

As much as she wanted to comfort their temporary savior Amber needed to get to Grandma. She put her bags down quickly.

"Madame, I must see to my Grandma. There are things she can't do alone."

"Oh, of course. Go, go!"

Amber hurried down the stairs to Grandma's room and closed the door. Grandma stood before the opulent mirror, her hands in tight fists.

"Should we do this now?" she asked nervously.

"We have no choice," Grandma replied. "We need to know what's happening and my father is the only one who can tell us."

Amber held up her hand then crept to the door.

"Is everything okay?" Madame Josephine asked through the ebony wood door.

"Yes Madame, everything is fine," Amber replied. "Thank you so much for allowing us to stay here. My grandmother must perform a few procedures that require privacy."

"I understand," Josephine said.

She listened to Madame walk away then turned back to Grandma.

"Okay, go ahead."

Grandma opened her hands, revealing the white power. She brought her pursed lips close to her palms then hesitated.

"I don't have much left," she said.

"We'll manage," Amber replied. "I know we will. I feel stronger here."

Grandma smiled. "You are home, Amber." She blew the dust into the mirror. The effect occurred much faster than in America or France. The image of her great grandfather appeared instantly and it was not an encouraging sight. He looked frailer than before, his garments almost swallowing him. He looked up at the mirror from his chair, his sunken eyes flickering as he forced a smile.

"My daughters," he whispered.

Grandma touched the mirror surface. "Baba, what happened?"

His smile grew wider. "Don't worry. I'll be fine. I had to do something that drained my power for a time but I will recover. The main concern is for you. Where are you?"

"We're in Dakar, Senegal," Amber answered.

Her great grandfather nodded. "Your journey is almost complete but you still have a long way to travel. The situation has changed."

"Yes, we know…baba," Amber said. "A woman is chasing us, a shape shifter. She came to us disguised as Bissau. We came to Dakar with her. We were able to get away but she's searching for us."

"She is Aisha, a shape-shifter," great-grandfather said. "Bagule sent her to stop you. Because she is not Maraibu she can travel through the Veil with no restrictions."

"Where is the real Bissau?" Amber asked.

"He is on his way, I hope," great grandfather said. "I passed to him much power to aid him. You must stay away from Aisha at all cost. She is capable of dangerous things."

Grandma grimaced. "That is why…"

He raised his hand. "Don't worry about me, child. I will recover. The most important thing now is that you and Amber leave Dakar as soon as possible. Aisha will find you if you stay."

"But where do we go?" Amber asked.

Great grandfather smiled. "Touch the mirror, Amber."

Amber looked at her grandmother.

"Go ahead, Amby," she urged.

Amber approached the mirror and placed her hand on the cool glass. Great grandfather sat up then reached out to her. Their palms met and she felt his warmth. It was if they were the same room. She tried to slip her fingers between his and was reminded that it was an image she looked at, nothing more.

"You have the power to come home," he said. "You have to let go of that last mote of doubt before you fully realize your potential. When you do, the path to Marai will be clear."

"How do I do that, baba?" she said. The word for father came from her lips easily, as if she'd spoke it all her life.

"It will come," he said. "The process has already begun."

Great grandfather took his hand away. Amber stepped away from the mirror with a new energy stirring in her chest. Her eyes widened.

"What did you give me?" she blurted.

Great grandfather smiled. "A little something to start you on your way. You hold more promise than I suspected, Amber. Rest now, both of you. The answers you seek are closer than you expect."

Great grandfather's image wavered. He raised his hand for a final goodbye, his appearance replaced by reflection. Amber turned to Grandma, her mind filled with hope and confusion.

"I don't understand," she said.

Grandma took her hand. "Baba is never wrong, Amby. Do as he says. Go to your room and rest. We'll let Madame Josephine wait on us for a time which she is so anxious to do. You'll need a clear mind to think about what we should do next."

"You'll have to help me," Amber said.

"Of course I will, but it's been a long time since I left Marai. The path I followed may no longer exist."

"I hope Bissau finds us," Amber mused.

"Think of him and he will," Grandma answered.

Grandma kissed her on the cheek. "I'm going to lie down. I suggest you do the same. Madame Josephine doesn't seem to be the type that will let us rest too long."

Amber giggled. "No, she doesn't."

Amber opened Grandma's door and met Madame Josephine standing in the hall, a nervous look on her face.

"Everything is perfect, isn't it?" she asked.

"Yes, Madame. Everything is fine."

Josephine placed her hand on her chest and exhaled. "*Bon.* I know that some travelers get sick when they visit other countries."

Amber gave Madame a reassuring smile. "She's fine, Madame. She just needs to rest, as I do."

"Of course, of course! Go to your room and relax. I will let you know when dinner is ready. And I assure you, it will be a feast indeed. Have you ever had Senegalese food?"

"No I haven't," Amber replied, trying to keep her apprehension from entering her voice.

Madame Josephine clapped her hands. "Then you are in for a treat. Our food is the best in all of West Africa. If you ask me, it is the best in the world!"

Madame Josephine followed Amber to her room then left once she was certain Amber was comfortable. Amber's room contained a private bathroom so she was able to slip out of her travel clothes and into her pajamas without leaving. As she washed her face she gazed at her reflection. Five days into her adventure and she was still trying to grasp this new reality. A whole world existed within her normal life and no one suspected it. How could that be? How could her parents live with her every day and not know something was different about her? Worse still, how did she not know?

As she scrubbed her face the necklace grew warm. Soon after she saw something in the mirror. She looked behind her; the door was still closed. Amber peered deeper into the mirror and the image came into focus. It was not the room behind her; it was a busy street filled with pedestrians and cars. It was Paris. She blinked her eyes and the image remained. In fact, it became clearer. How was this happening? She had none of grandmother's mystical dust. Maybe some had lingered on her clothing, somehow transforming her mirror into a bridge. But this was not her great grandfather's chambers. She remembers his words then. Was this what he was speaking of? Then she touched her necklace. It was the necklace!

A young, handsome man entered her view, a man whose face was familiar to her.

"Bissau," she said.

The man stopped and looked about. Amber's hand flew to her mouth.

The man turned back and forth, staring into the crowd around him. People gave him curious glances as they avoided him.

Amber smiled. This was amazing!

"Bissau," she said firmly.

Bissau hurried to a café and sat at a vacant table. A waiter appeared and he waved him away.

"Who speaks to me this way? Is this you, Aisha? I swear before the ancestors I will…"

"No, this is not Aisha. This is Amber."

Bissau sat up straight. "Amber? How…no, that does not matter. Where are you?"

"I'm with Grandma. We are in Dakar, Senegal."

Bissau stood quickly. "Stay where you are. I am coming!"

"We can't stay," Amber replied. "Aisha came with us disguised as you. I was able to see through her façade when we arrived in Dakar. We escaped but she is looking for us."

"What are you going to do?"

Amber closed her eyes and searched her mind. The answer that came to her wasn't what she expected, but she accepted it. Her great grandfather told her to trust her thoughts, so she would.

"We are going to Marai," she said.

Bissau's eyes went wide. "How can you? You don't know the way."

"I'll find it," she answered.

"Give me one day," Bissau said. "I'll find a way to get to Dakar. Just one more day."

"I'll try, Bissau. Baba trusts you, so I will, too. Come quickly."

Bissau smiled. "I will."

He ran to the curb and flagged down a taxi. Amber watched him enter the vehicle then it sped away. The mirror image faded and she looked at herself once again. She suddenly felt exhausted, the strain of the day catching up with her. She barely made it to the bed before collapsing into the soft mattress and falling immediately to sleep.

"Wake up. Wake up, child!" Madame Josephine said through the door. "Dinner will be served soon. You don't want to miss it!"

Madame Josephine's voice was as startling as an alarm. Amber awoke slurping. She rolled on her back and rubbed her forehead. Her head throbbed. She sat up with her eyes still closed.

"Amber?"

The male voice startled her and her eyes snapped open. Bissau stood in the corner of her room, a smile on his face. Amber covered her mouth as she screamed into her hand. They stared at each other for what seem liked hours, Amber working to control her emotions.

"It's okay," he said in heavily accented French. "I assure you I am the real Bissau. Aisha wouldn't be foolish enough to use the same disguise again. Besides, you could see through it. You know I am who I say I am."

Amber eased her hand from her mouth. "How did you get here?"

Bissau pointed at the mirror. "It is how I traveled to France as well. Master Jakada shared his talents with me which allows me to travel through the portals. When you contacted me you opened a new path."

"Amber?" Madame Josephine's voice cut through her haze.

"I have to eat," Amber said. "Stay here."

Bissau smiled. "Where else would I go?"

He lifted his head and sniffed. "It smells good."

"Are you hungry?"

Bissau rubbed his stomach. "Very."

"I'll see if I can sneak something back." She began to get out the bed then realized she wore only her night gown.

"I have to change," she said.

Bissau looked puzzled for a moment then his eyes widened. "I'm sorry."

"Go into the bathroom," she said.

Confusion twisted Bissau's face. Amber pointed at the bathroom.

"Ahh!" Bissau went into the bathroom and shut the door. Amber dressed quickly then went downstairs. Madame Josephine and Grandma waited for her, both women smiling at her as she descended.

"You are a princess," Madame Josephine said.

"Yes she is," Grandma agreed.

The three of them proceeded to the dining room, an elaborate space with a beautiful and intimate table resting under a pearl white ceiling fan. The man who served as chauffeur now served them as waiter.

"Follow me," he said. He led them to their seats, and then disappeared into the next room. He returned with bowls of soup which were delicious. Soon afterwards the man returned with bowls containing their meals.

"I didn't know what you would prefer, so I had my cook prepare a variety."

Miss Josephine pointed at the first bowl.

"This is yassa, chicken simmered in onion with garlic, mustard, and lemon sauce. It is my favorite."

She pointed at the next bowl. "This is maafe, seasoned beef cooked with vegetables in a peanut sauce. And this' – she pointed at the last bowl – is Thiéboudienne. No visit to Senegal is complete without tasting our national meal."

Miss Josephine returned to her seat. "*Bon apetit, mes soeurs!*"

Madame Josephine smiled broadly as Amber and Grandma ate their meals.

"You know I have been to America quite a few times," she said.

"Really?" Amber reluctantly placed her fork down. The food was so delicious she didn't want to stop eating.

"Yes, dear! I used to visit New York often with my husband. He had an import/export business there. We also have many relatives in the city. It's the only place in America where you can get decent Senegalese food."

"I've been to New York, too," Amber answered. "I wish I'd known there were Senegalese restaurants there. I would have asked my parents to take me."

Josephine clapped her hands. "The food is good, no?"

Grandma looked up from her plate smiling. "Very."

Josephine raised her hands in praise. "Then I am a satisfied host."

"Have you ever been to Georgia?" Amber asked.

"Ahh yes, Georgia! I have been to Atlanta. They call it the Black Mecca."

Amber giggled then quickly covered her mouth. "Yes, some folks call it that."

"It is a very beautiful city," Josephine commented. "Very green and the people are friendly. If they had Senegalese food it would be perfect!"

The ladies laughed like old friends. Despite her gaiety Amber could sense Miss Josephine's sorrow.

"So, what happened to your husband?" she asked.

The light in Josephine's eyes faded. Grandma cleared her throat for Amber's attention. Amber looked her way and Grandma barely shook her head. Amber did a slight nod in return.

"My husband fell ill a few years ago and never recovered," she answered.

"What did he suffer from?" Amber asked.

Miss Josephine placed her hands in her lap, her eyes downcast. "Malaria. We were on a trip to Nigeria when he fell ill. He lingered for a long time."

"What about your children?"

"They live in America. I visit them sometimes, but they have children of their own. There is little time for mama these days."

Grandma reached out and touched Josephine's hand. "Children do not cherish their elders as they should these days," she said. "It is only when they are about to part when they realized what they truly possess."

Amber looked into her Grandma's glistening eyes. She realized that this was a conversation touching them all, not only Miss Josephine. Grandma left home long ago, losing the connection with her parents and now she sat with her while her own parents vacationed without her. Though part of her reason was much more that a selfish whim she realized she was just as guilty as Miss Josephine's children.

"So, this is why I entertain," Miss Josephine concluded, her bright smile returning. "If I can't be of any use to my children, at least I can help people visiting my wonderful country."

They finished their meals. Amber was handing her plate to the server when she remembered Bissau.

"Miss Josephine, could I have something to take to my room? I tend to get a little hungry during the night and I don't want to stumble about in an unfamiliar house."

Miss Josephine pinched her chin. "I usually don't allow such a thing, but you have been such wonderful guests. I'll have Bundu prepare something for you."

Grandma looked at her with narrow eyes and Amber looked back with assurance.

"Thank you, Miss Josephine. Dinner was wonderful."

"It was," Grandma agreed.

Amber walked Grandma back to her room.

"What's going on, child?" she asked.

"Bissau is in my room," Amber revealed.

She felt Grandma tense. "How did he get there?"

"Through the mirror. I think I summoned him."

Grandma nodded. "You are coming into your own. Baba was right."

"I don't know what to do," she said. "I can't hide him forever."

"You don't have to," Grandma replied. "With Bissau here we can plan our journey to Marai. It will only be one night."

Amber frowned. She had a problem with Bissau sleeping in her room.

Grandma gave her a knowing grin.

"Don't worry, Bissau is not like the boys you know. First of all, he is a man of Marai, an honorable and courteous person. Second, you are his mentor's great granddaughter. He wouldn't dare disgrace himself. Third, you're stronger than you know. You wouldn't let him."

Amber's nervousness wasn't based on Bissau's behavior. It was based on her own feelings. Bissau was a handsome boy, and he seemed so sure of himself. Grandma called him a man, and in a way, he was.

"Go upstairs, child," Grandma urged. "You'll be fine, trust me."

Amber took longer than normal making sure Grandma was comfortable.

"Go on, child," Grandma said. "Bissau is probably starving."

Amber kissed Grandma's cheek then left the room. She took her time up the stairs. Bundu waited for her at the room entrance.

"I brought you fruit, water and bread," he said. "Is there anything else you require?"

"No, thank you Bundu," she answered.

Bundu nodded. "Have a pleasant night, mademoiselle."

Amber took the tray and Bundu opened the door. Bissau was nowhere to be seen to her relief. No sooner did she close the door did he emerge from the bathroom.

"I'm sorry it took so long," Amber stammered. "Miss Josephine is a very talkative person."

Bissau's eyes widened. "You speak Bambara!"

Amber hadn't notice the change. Apparently her gift adjusted involuntarily.

"I guess I do."

She extended the tray to Bissau. He took the tray and sat on the edge of the bed, eating gingerly despite his hunger. Amber sat in the chair before the vanity, watching him as he ate. She was a swirl of emotions, some of them unnerving. She wasn't a wall flower by any means; she'd had a few boyfriends with an emphasis on the boy. But Bissau was different. She stopped her musing and covered her mouth to hide her grin. What was she thinking? She didn't even know him!

Bissau finished his meal and smiled at her.

"Thank you, Amber."

She took the tray, their eyes meeting.

"I guess you'll have to sleep in my room."

Bissau's expression turned serious. "I don't wish to cause you any discomfort. I can go back to Paris and return later."

"How can you…oh." They both looked at the mirror.

"No, you can stay here," Amber finally said.

"I'll sleep on the floor," Bissau said immediately.

Amber didn't argue. She stripped the sheet from the bed and handed it to Bissau. Afterwards she took her things and retreated into the bathroom.

"There's a man in my room," she whispered. "There's a man in my room!"

She fumbled through her night time ritual, her hands trembling. When she was done she looked at herself and frowned.

"This look ain't working."

She shook her head. Her dreams were interfering with her reality, but then again, her reality at the moment was like a dream. She rustled around in her make-up bag until she found her phone. Her fingers flew nimbly across the keypad as she texted Jasmine.

"Girl, you awake?"

Amber sent the text before she remembered the time difference. It was probably early morning in Atlanta.

"I am now," the return text read. *"How's the beach?"*

Amber hesitated before replying. She couldn't tell her parents where she was. What made her think she could tell Jasmine?

Her fingers hovered for a moment. Shoot, Jasmine was her best friend, her sister by another mother. Her fingertips attacked the keypad.

"I'm in Dakar, Senegal."

"Where's that?"

"Africa."

"Girl, don't play with me."

"I'm for real! I'm in Dakar, Senegal and there's a man in my room."

For what seemed like forever there was no response. Amber wasn't surprised. Jasmine probably thought she was crazy. As she was about to put her phone away it chirped.

"Somebody done kidnapped you!"

Amber pinched her lips to keep from laughing out loud.

"Naw! It ain't like that. I'm with my Grandma. It's a long story. I'll tell you when I get back."

A shiver ran through her as a dark thought popped in her head. *If I get back.*

"Who is this man in your room?"

"He's my protector."

"Is he fine?"

"Yeah, and he's cute too but it ain't about that."

"It's always about that."

"You're so nasty."

"Look who's talking. I'm not in Africa with a man in my room."

"Girl, you crazy! I'll hit you back later. Peace!"

"Be careful! Peace!"

Amber shoved her phone back into her bag and inspected herself one last time. She frowned; she wished she looked older. There was too much girl in her face and not enough woman. She took a deep breath and stepped back into her room.

Bissau was sound asleep on the floor. Amber smiled; what was she thinking? She wouldn't know the first thing to do. Relief and embarrassment took hold and she giggled. It had been a long day and would be an interesting tomorrow. It was time she got to bed.

CHAPTER TWENTY-ONE

Aisha kicked the garbage can across the alley and screamed. She struck out with her fists, imagining Bissau's face as the target for her frustration. A sound distracted her; she turned to see a group of people staring at her. She grinned maliciously then before the eyes of her unwanted spectators she transformed into a huge grey hyena. Her maniacal laugh sent them all scurrying away; Aisha transformed back to her true self before exiting the other end of the alley.

She underestimated Amber. Whatever powers she possessed manifested the moment they landed in the Motherland. She had been overconfident when she knew better and now the girl and her mother were lost in Dakar. A quick sweep of the local hotels revealed they were not checked in. They were clever; they knew it would be the first place she searched. They weren't familiar with the city, so they wouldn't take a chance in seeking a stranger for help. Aisha was dumbfounded. Where would a person begin to look for another in this world? She would have to start with her own knowledge then go from there. In Marai each folk claimed its own section of the city. She would look for the American section of the city, if one existed. That would be where they would most likely go if they didn't choose a hotel. Aisha spotted a man dressed in a large purple shirt and loose pants striding down the street towards her. There was a smile on his face; Aisha smiled backed then approached him.

"Excuse me sir," she said in her sweetest tone. "Where would I find the American compound?"

The man looked puzzled. "American compound? There is no...oh, you must mean the American Embassy."

"Yes, that is what I meant."

The man scratched his chin. "It's a long way from here. Come, I'm walking to my car. I'll take you there."

"Merci, monsieur! Merci!"

Aisha followed the man to a dusty vehicle. She was used to automobiles now, so she climbed into the passenger side. They pulled away quickly.

"What's your name?" the man asked.

"Aisha."

"Well Aisha, your Mama should have taught you never to get in a car with a stranger."

The man's sinister grin was barely on his face when Aisha snatched her wicked dagger from her clothes and pressed the tip into his neck. It was her turn to grin.

"No, sir. You should be old enough to know not to try to take advantage of pretty young girls. Now take me to this American embassy."

The man's fearful eyes drifted down to the blade. "You won't do it. I'm driving!"

Aisha pressed the knife into his neck just enough to draw blood. The man whimpered.

"The embassy, fool!" she spat.

The man drove to a building that flew a red, white and blue flag decorated with stars. Aisha leaned closed to her reluctant chauffeur then kissed him on the cheek.

"Thank you for the ride," she whispered.

She nicked his neck with her knife as she exited the car. The man yelled at her and shook his fist. Aisha had already forgotten him.

The military man at the door greeted her with a smile before looking over her shoulder at the irate man.

"Is there a problem, ma'am?" he asked.

"No sir, but you are very kind to ask."

Aisha glanced over her shoulder as her involuntary ride sped away.

"I hope you can help me, monsieur," she said. "My friends from America came to visit me today but it seems I lost them at the airport. I think they would come to the embassy if they were lost."

The guard looked at her skeptically. "There were two Americans that came to the embassy earlier today. You say they are your friends?"

"Yes, monsieur."

"Yet you missed them at the airportthen come here seeking them?"

"I must make a confession," she said. "My friends would not know me if they saw me. I was to meet them at the airport to assist them in their travels. They apparently grew impatient."

"They've made other arrangements," the guard said gruffly. "Have a nice day, ma'am."

"Please, monsieur, I must find them!" Aisha pleaded.

The guard studied her a few moments before answering.

"You can talk with the receptionist," he said.

"Merci, monsieur. Merci."

Aisha went to the receptionist. The woman confirmed that Amber and Alake had indeed come to the embassy, but she wasn't at liberty to say where they were staying.

Aisha thanked her then left the embassy. So the duo had taken refuge in a local home. It would seem to be a good move, but there were few homes in Dakar that could provide two lodgers the comfort of a hotel. Her search would not be as difficult as Amber had surmised. She had no doubt she would see them very soon. She found another alley, ran then leaped into the air, her arms spread wide. She transformed into a falcon, a cry of joy escaping her mouth. Of all the creatures she could be, the birds of prey were her favorite. Their powerful bodies combined with their keen sight and ultimate mobility fascinated her. If there was any creature she could remain for the rest of her life, it would be such a beast.

She beat her wings, climbing higher over Dakar. It did not take her long to find the city section she sought. A line of mansions rimmed the oceanside, houses resembling the lineage of Marai. She circled, seeking obvious signs of where Amber and the others would be but there was none. They were smarter than that, but the most intelligent person can make mistakes, as Bissau proved in Paris. She descended and found a perch on a nearby office building. The mid-day heat did not bother her; she was a child of the desert and the falcon she chose to be was well adapted to the high heat. Now was time for patience. She felt sure she was in the right place. She would soon have what she wanted.

It was dusk when she saw it. A mystical flash rose from a sector of town south of her. She jumped from her perch, flying as fast as she could to the source before it waned. Someone used nyama near-by and she was sure she knew who. Despite her speed by the time she reached the source of the flash it had dissipated. Two homes filled her view, both splendid compared to the other homes in Dakar. There was only one way she could find which house was which. She transformed into her human female form, this time wearing the clothes of a local. She waited until darkness settled on the city before walking to the door of the first home. She knocked for a long while before giving up and proceeding to the next house. Aisha knocked then took on a sad expression as she heard someone approach. The door swung wide and was filled by a large man with a disapproving face.

"What do you want?" he barked.

"Something to eat," she replied.

"No beggars here," he said. "Now go before I call the police."

"Just a little something," she pleaded.

The man grabbed her shirt. "Didn't you hear me? Be gone. You'll disturb Miss Josephine and her guests!"

Aisha's eyes narrowed and she smiled. "Of course, I will."

Aisha's knee sank into the man's stomach. He dropped her and she landed on her feet. She stepped over the groaning man into the house.

"Bundu, who is it at such a late hour?"

Aisha saw a light appear on her left. Another light appeared on her right. She looked right and a saw a woman she did not recognize walking toward her as she tied her house robe belt.

"Who are you, child?" The woman demanded. "What is the meaning of...Bundu!"

The second door opened. A woman stepped out, a woman whose face was very familiar. The woman saw Aisha and her hands flew to her mouth.

A third door flew open at the top of the stairs. Bissau rushed out, his face twisted in anger. He jumped from the top of the stairs. Aisha grinned.

She waited until Bissau was almost on the floor when she transformed back into the falcon and flew by him to the room. When she transformed she stood before Amber.

"Your journey is over," Aisha announced.

Amber stumbled back. The necklace about her neck glowed with a strange light.

"That necklace will be mine once I'm done with you!"

She struck at Amber's neck and was shocked when the girl blocked her blow. Her foot flashed out and Amber blocked it as well. She almost laughed when Amber punched at her face until she realized the punch was a feint. She barely avoided the swinging elbow meant for her jaw.

"You have some wrestling skills," Aisha said. "Your grandmother taught you well."

Aisha glanced behind her; Bissau and Aisha's grandmother were running up the stairs.

"Time to end this!"

Aisha reached for her pouch. Amber kicked her elbow and her arm fell limp.

"Damn you, girl. I'll…"

Bright light filled her vision as Amber's elbow crashed against her head then everything went dark. When she opened her eyes the back of her head throbbed and Bissau, Amber and her grandmother were entering the mirror inside the room.

"No you don't!" Aisha yelled.

She jumped at the mirror. Bissau reemerged and slammed into her, knocking her to the floor. She tried to stand but Bissau pulled her back down.

"We have unfinished business, shape shifter!" he snarled.

"Then it will remain unfinished!" Aisha reached for her pouch again. Bissau dodged her and ran toward the mirror. Aisha smiled; as soon as he opened his portal she would follow him. He did no such thing. Instead he picked up a nearby chair and smashed the mirror. Aisha screamed then fell onto Bissau, pummeling him with hands, feet, elbows and knees.

"Upstairs!" she heard a female voice yell. "They're upstairs!"

Aisha halted her assault on Bissau. He lay unconscious at her feet, his beautiful face beginning to swell. She ran to the edge of the stairs and saw four uniformed men climbing up to her followed by the woman and her butler. She hissed in anger; she was back to where she started. But at least this time she had a lead. She hurried over to Bissau, grasping his arms with her hands. What she was about to do would weaken her, but she needed him, at least until she could locate Amber and her grandmother again. The transformation took longer than normal; once she was done she was a falcon again and Bissau was a mouse in her talons. She flew upward as the uniformed men reached the top of the stairs then glided out of the door into the humid night.

CHAPTER TWENTY-TWO

Amber awoke cramped and incredibly hot. She tried to move but Grandma sagged against her.

"Grandma? Grandma?"

Grandma didn't answer. Amber pushed against the hard surface pinning her in place. It gave; she sighed and then shifted, placing her feet on the opposite wall then pushed with all her strength. The wall against her back cracked. She gathered her strength again then pushed. She was rewarded with a loud crack then she fell. Her back and head smacked against a hard surface then she blacked out. When she came to Grandma lay on top of her still unconscious. She looked up into a dozen faces, their words assaulting her as she lay hurt.

"Someone help them."

"Help, them? Where did they come from?"

"Get a doctor! The elder one is injured!"

Hands grasped her then lifted her to her feet. A man covered in blue garb carried her grandmother; Amber stumbled alongside a woman covered in a brightly patterned dress with a headscarf covering her braided hair. The buildings were all the same color and sand was everywhere.

"Where are we?" she asked. She didn't know which language she used.

The woman gave her a kind smile. "Timbuktu."

Amber and the woman followed the blue robed man into the only modern building in Timbuktu. The woman standing before them was dressed like someone from Atlanta; short khaki pants and hiking boots with a sweat-stained tank top. Her reddish-brown hair was tied up over her head. She smiled at Amber, her honey colored face creased with wrinkles. Her smile faded when she saw Grandma.

"Bring her here," she said.

They followed the woman into the next room. An examination bed rested against the opposite wall accompanied by a grey metal cabinet. The room, to Amber's relief, was air conditioned. The man laid Grandma on the bed as the woman went to her desk, taking out her stethoscope from the top drawer. She smiled as he hurried to the bed.

"What's your name, honey?" she asked.

"Amber."

"I'm Dr. Ann Dunaway. You can call me Dr. Ann. What happened, Amber?"

"We fell."

The woman's eyes narrowed with suspicion. "Uh huh."

She felt Grandma's head. "Doesn't seem to be any obvious injuries."

She placed her stethoscope to Grandma's chest then listened.

"Heart rate seems fine."

The woman nodded at the robed man and his companion and they left the room, both giving Amber a curious glance on their way out.

"Looks like your grandmother may have a concussion," the doctor said. "I'll keep an eye on her until she comes to then do a more thorough examination. Now let's take a look at you."

"I'm okay," Amber said.

"You just fell a long way," Ann replied. "You are not okay."

Ann shined her pen light into Amber's eyes then listened to her chest. She examined her head then took off her gloves and sat opposite her.

"Your grandmother will be fine, but she can't be moved for a while. I'm going to contact a colleague in Djenne. He has more experience with head injuries."

Amber's relief forced tears in her eyes. "Thank you so much!"

Ann shook her head. "You're lucky you had your accident today. This is my last day in Timbuktu. The local doctor his good, but he's not me."

Dr. Ann flashed a confident smile. "Now I have a question. How did you two get here?"

Amber looked away from Dr. Ann as she tried to come up with an explanation. She failed.

"I don't know," she finally said.

Ann rubbed her chin thoughtfully. "Looks like you may be suffering from short tern amnesia. Head trauma can sometimes affect short term memory."

Amber brightened. "That's probably it."

Dr. Ann still seemed curious. "I've been here a week and no one has mentioned either one of you. The people who brought you in say you fell from the sky."

Amber laughed nervously. "An attic maybe, but not the sky. I think we would be in worse shape."

"I've seen stranger things," Ann replied. "A boat is coming for me tomorrow. You can come with me and sort things out later."

"No!" Amber blurted. "Ah, there's something we have to do here."

Ann folded her arms. "The plot thickens. Well, the offer stands if you change your mind. Everything depends on your grandmother's recovery."

Dr. Ann stood. "Stay here with your grandmother. I have rounds to make in the city. There's water and something to eat in the fridge in the other room."

"You're very trusting," Amber commented.

Ann smiled. "You look like a good kid. Besides, where are you going to go?"

You have no idea, Amber thought.

She waited until Dr. Ann left the room before going to Grandma. She looked like she was sleeping. Amber let herself cry for a moment before reining in her emotions. She had to get them out of this office and back to finding Marai. She had no idea what happened to Bissau, but it was becoming obvious that as cute as he was, Bissau was not going to get them there. He had his hands full keeping the woman trying to stop them at bay. It was up to her and Grandma to get to Marai.

She went to the mirror then looked at her reflection. She was dirty and her perm was growing out. A laugh burst from her lips.

"I'm stranded in Timbuktu and I'm worried about my perm?"

She took a pinch of Grandma's concoction and flicked it onto the mirror. The silvery substance swirled, making her dizzy for a moment. An image finally solidified but it was not the image she hoped. It was a street scene of a city she did not recognize and she had no desire to go to another unknown adventure. The next time she entered a mirror she wanted to emerge in her great grandfather's chamber.

"Amby? Baby, where are you?"

Amber rushed to Grandma's side then clutched her hand.

"I'm right here Grandma, right here."

Grandma faced Amber and smiled. It was the sweetest sight Amber had seen in days and it almost made her cry again.

"Where are we?" she asked, her voice weak yet hopeful.

"Timbuktu," Amber said.

Grandma's smile grew. "We are close then. I knew it. I could feel it."

"How close?"

"Very. Marai is one of the three Sisters. The others are Djenne and Timbuktu."

Grandma looked about the room. "Where is Bissau?"

"He went back to stop the woman," Amber said with an edge in her voice.

Grandma shifted in her bed. "I hope we see him again."

Grandma's words startled Amber. It never occurred to her that Bissau might be killed by the woman pursuing them. As a matter of fact, it never occurred to her that the woman might try to kill her.

"I have to find another mirror," Amber concluded. "Maybe this one will take us to Marai."

"No, it won't," Grandma said. "Marai possesses a barrier that makes it invisible to the rest of the world. It keeps the world out, but it also keeps the Maraibu in. No nyama can easily penetrate it."

"Then how did Bissau get outside?"

Grandma looked thoughtful. "I suspect it took my father great effort to get him through. But we don't need it now. I know the way from here."

The bottom slowly disappeared from Amber's stomach.

"I hope Bissau is alright."

Grandma grasped her hand. "I hope so too, but Bissau knew the risks when he came to find us. Whatever his fate, he will be satisfied with it."

The thought made her sick to her stomach.

"I don't feel good," she said.

Grandma stroked her head. "It's okay, Amber. I'm sure he's all right. In the meantime, we must be on our way."

"You're too hurt to travel."

"I am now, but I'll get better. When I am we'll have to move as soon as possible."

"I don't know what to do!" Amber exclaimed.

"Yes you do, child," Grandma said. "Let your instincts guide you."

Amber calmed with Grandma's soothing words. She closed her eyes and concentrated on their situation.

"We need clothes," she said. "We left ours in Dakar."

"You'll have to go to the market," Grandma said.

"By myself?"

Grandma chuckled. "Of course. Your language ability will help. And go with your instinct. Choose what you feel is right."

Dr. Ann interrupted their conversation.

"So my patient is conscious. Excellent!"

Amber moved aside as the doctor went to work. She flashed her pen light in Grandma's eyes and took her vitals.

"Seems you do have a slight concussion," Dr. Ann finally said. "The fall didn't hurt you as much as I suspected. How old are you?"

"Eighty," Grandma replied.

Dr. Ann rubbed her chin. "Well, all I have to say is I hope I'm in as good shape as you when I'm eighty."

"It's the local climate," Grandma joked. "It suits me."

Amber looked at her Grandma and her eyebrows rose. She did look younger. Grandma looked back at her, her brows raised as well.

"Dr. Ann, is there somewhere I can go to find some clothes?"

Dr. Ann's curious expression returned. "You don't have any clothes?"

"We lost our luggage on the way here," Amber lied.

"There are a few stores at the market, but you won't find much as far as the latest fashions. This is Timbuktu."

"Something local would be fine," Grandma said.

Dr. Ann shrugged. "Okay, but you're not going anywhere. I'll get Pemba to take Amber. She helps me around the city and I think she's about your age."

"Thank you," Amber said.

As soon as Dr. Ann left the room Amber shuffled over to Grandma.

"You do look younger!"

"I feel younger too," Grandma replied. "That's how I know I'm closer to home. Marai reaches out to me."

"This is amazing," Amber exclaimed.

"And dangerous," Grandma added. "The sooner we leave the better."

"Dr. Ann is leaving tomorrow. She said we can go with her."

Grandma shook her head. "She's heading in the wrong direction. We'll stay here a few more days to see if Bissau comes. If not we'll set out on our own."

"With what?" Amber asked. "We don't have a car or anything!"

Grandma smiled. "We'll take camels."

"Camels?" Amber shivered.

Amber was about to protest when Dr. Ann entered the room accompanied by a girl with ebony skin and dancing eyes. She wore a pair of worn jeans and a Boston Celtics t-shirt with matching green sneakers. She smiled at Grandma and Amber.

"Amber, this is Pemba," Dr. Ann said. "She'll take you to the market."

Pemba rushed Amber then gave her a tight hug.

"Welcome to Timbuktu," she said in English with a heavy accent. She grabbed Amber's hand then pulled her toward the door.

"Be careful with her, Pemba!" the doctor called out.

"I will!"

Pemba looked at Amber with a big smile. "You are the first girl I've met from America!"

Amber smiled back, a bit overwhelmed by Pemba's enthusiasm. "You're the first girl I've met from Timbuktu."

Pemba's eyes widened. "You speak Mandika!"

"I guess so," Amber replied.

"Good! You can tell me all about America, and I will tell you all about Timbuktu!"

Pemba led Amber out of the doctor's home and into the dusty streets of Timbuktu.

CHAPTER TWENTY-THREE

Bissau winced as he struck the pavement. His body ached as he transformed from rodent to man again. When his eyes cleared Aisha loomed over him, knife in hand. She looked angry.

"No more games, Bissau!" she spat. "Where did you send them?"

Bissau said nothing. If there was one thing he knew, it was that Aisha would not kill him. She would hurt him, however. Of that he was sure.

She confirmed his thoughts by kicking him in the stomach. He doubled over, grasping her foot then twisting hard. She fell and then rolled with his motion to prevent him from breaking her ankle, the knife flying free as she threw her hands out to catch her fall. Bissau was on his feet and running before she struck the ground. By the time she gathered herself he was out of the narrow alley and onto the main street. No sooner had he relaxed did two men dressed in black fatigues and red berets appeared before him.

"We've been looking for you," one of them said.

They spun him around then handcuffed him. He looked into the alley. Aisha stumbled in the opposite direction, favoring the leg he twisted. Bissau managed a smile before the men spun him around again then led him to their automobile.

"Inside," the other man barked.

Bissau entered without a struggle, grateful for the moment's rest. He had time to reassess his situation. Amber and Alake were in Timbuktu now. He was not confident Alake would get them to Marai from there. His problem would be reaching them. He'd broken Nana Josephine's mirror to prevent the shape shifter from following but it also prevented him from doing the same. He would have to find another mirror as soon as possible.

By the time they reached the building of the constables Bissau had decided what he was going to say. The car door opened and the stern duo pulled him out then led him inside the building. He shook when the unnaturally chilled air touched his skin. The building teemed with other officers, each of them stealing a glance at him and shaking their heads. He knew the gesture and the look. It was one he suffered many times from those of lineage in Marai before Jele Jakada took him in as an apprentice. Their opinion did not matter. What he thought of himself was most important.

They led him to a table in the center of the room then shoved him into a chair. Nana Josephine sat opposite him, worry clear on her face. His captors sat before him; another man dressed in a white short-sleeve shirt and black pants appeared then sat before him with some type of box. He was an elder, his head graced with gray hair, his eyes aided by a pair of glasses.

"State your name," one of the uniformed men said. He spoke a language that seemed similar to Bambara. Bissau could understand him well enough.

"Bissau Kieta," he said.

The elder stood then folded his arms across his chest. "Okay, Bissau. What were you doing hiding in Mademoiselle Josephine's home in the room of her female guest?"

Bissau sat up in his seat. He'd decided he would do the only thing he could do. He would tell the truth.

"I am Bissau Kieta, acolyte of Jele Jakada of Marai. I was sent by him to find his daughter Alake and her granddaughter Amber and bring them back to Marai."

The elder looked at the constables. They shrugged. Nana Josephine covered her mouth with her well-manicured hand.

"Are you crazy?" the elder said. "Marai is a myth. Don't play with us, boy!"

Bissau ignored his threat. "I traveled through my teacher's mirror to Paris where I was to meet them. Instead I encountered the shape shifter, who had taken my place to fool the women. She enchanted me with her powder which left me paralyzed. When I recovered I followed the three of them to Dakar."

The room was silent. All the other uniformed men had gathered around the table to listen to Bissau. The elder rubbed his forehead as the crowd grew. He slammed his hand on the table, startling Nana Josephine.

"You expect us to believe this mess?" he shouted.

Bissau stared into the man's eyes. He decided this elder did not deserve his respect. He pointed at the constables.

"You saw a woman transform into a falcon, fly upstairs then become a woman again. You saw two women jump through a mirror. You saw me fight the woman who turned me into a mouse, turn back into a falcon then fly both of us out of the house. You saw all of this and you don't believe what I am saying now?"

The uniformed men eyes shifted. Nana Josephine bit her fist then looked away. The others stared at the two men, questions obvious in their eyes.

The elder turned to Nana Josephine.

"Is this true?" he asked.

Nana Josephine cleared her throat before answering.

"Well, I really can't say that it's not."

The elder rolled his eyes. "Why do I always get the crazy ones?"

He rushed to Bissau's side of the table, took off the handcuffs then lifted him out of his chair by his shirt collar.

"Get out!" he barked. "Get out of my office and get out of Dakar!"

Bissau cut the elder a mean glance then hurried from the building. He'd gambled and he'd won but he wasn't going to press his luck. He would leave Dakar as soon as he figured out how.

"Bissau, wait!"

Bissau cringed when he heard Nana Josephine voice. He walked faster.

"Bissau, please wait. I can help you!"

Bissau turned to see Nana Josephine running as fast as she fashionably could. He sighed then waited for her to catch up to him.

"I don't think you can help me, nana," he said.

"You travel through the mirrors," she said.

Bissau looked hard at the woman. Unlike the constables, she believed what he said. The constables just wanted to be rid of him so they wouldn't have to explain to their superiors what they saw.

"Yes, I do," he finally said.

"When my husband was alive he used to collect mirrors," she replied. "Most of them were from Europe or America, but there were a few from African countries."

"Go on," he said.

"I understand everything now," Nana Josephine said. "I was meant to take your friends in, and you were meant to find them. Now I think I am meant to help you find them again. Come, come!"

Bissau didn't move. What was this woman talking about? She sounded as strange to him as he knew he sounded to the constables.

Nana Josephine looked back at him.

"Come now, boy! We must hurry!"

"Yes, nana," he replied. He followed her to her automobile. He had no idea how he was going to locate Amber and Alake again, so following Nana Josephine wouldn't hurt. It would give him more time to come up with a better plan.

They rode back to Nana Josephine's house. Bissau looked about before going inside to make sure the shape shifter wasn't nearby. He followed Nana Josephine up the stairs to a room beside the one he and Amber had shared. The thought of them in the room together gave him a brief moment of pleasure and embarrassment. He had to admit that Master Jakada's granddaughter was an attractive woman. If he was horro, a person of noble lineage, he would raise loloba and approach Jele Jakada with a proposal of marriage. He smiled; it

141

would please him greatly to be related to the Jele. But he was not of the lineage to make such a gesture. Even if he became a great mage under Jakada's guidance his lineage could not be ignored. It was best he set his mind on tangible goals, like finding Amber and Alake.

Miss Josephine hesitated before opening the door.

"My husband bought this mirror in Djenne. The person who sold it to him said it once belonged to Sonni Ali. When Sonni Ali died it was passed on to Askia Muhammad. You know that some claim Sonni Ali possessed powers beyond those we know."

Bissau nodded. Jele Jakada taught of the men of which she spoke; he was their contemporary.

"Once we brought it home strange things began to occur so we locked it away," Miss Josephine said.

The antique door creaked as Miss Josephine opened it then stepped away. Bissau entered the room, enveloped by stale humid air. Rich dust covered furniture filled the room, each piece placed strategically around a large mirror standing on the floor and reaching to the ceiling. Thick ebony wood carved with stylized shapes of men and animals framed the glass. Bissau immediately sensed the nyama the mirror possessed as he neared. He grinned as he walked closer; Miss Josephine had not related the entire story. The only way such an object could exist undetected by him, Amber or Alake meant that the room had been sealed with protective spells. He looked back at the door. Miss Josephine peeked into the room, her eyes revealing her fear…and knowledge.

Bissau reached the mirror. He ran his fingers across the surface and warm bolts of static followed them. This was indeed a very powerful mirror. He reached into his pocket; there was very little powder remaining, but with this mirror it might be enough. He placed his fingers against the mirror then blew. The mirror surface wavered then swirled. Bissau stepped away as images appeared, blurry at first then eventually taking form.

"By the ancestors!" he gasped.

A stream of cities passed before his eyes, some ancient and others unlike any he'd ever seen. Marai appeared for a second in its current splendor then was replaced by an image whose geography was familiar but its buildings strange and beautiful. It took Bissau a moment to recognize the city. It was Timbuktu.

"There!" he shouted and the image stopped froze. Bissau didn't know what to do. On a whim he extended his hand toward the surface. He moved his hand and the image moved as well. A broad smile came to his face as he moved his hands rapidly. He stopped at the marketplace, moving his hands slowly, studying the faces as well as he could among the crowd. And then he saw her. She stood out among the brightly dressed residents of Timbuktu, her western garb like a signal light. She followed another woman through the throng, stopping at different stalls to peruse the clothing offered.

"You have a powerful mirror, nana," Bissau said.

He turned to Miss Josephine and met her nervous smile.

"You found them?" Her face was hopeful.

"Yes I have."

She pointed at the mirror. "And you will go to them through the mirror?"

Bissau nodded.

Miss Josephine rushed to him and gave him a motherly hug. Bissau's eyes widened in surprised then he settled into the embrace. It had been a long time since anyone held him this way and it was soothing.

"Merci beacoup, Miss Josephine," he said.

"Go to them," she whispered. "Go now before I cry."

Bissau stepped toward the mirror.

"Keep this room locked, nana. Others may come looking for this mirror."

Miss Josephine nodded.

Bissau smiled. "Don't worry. You are under my protection now."

He bowed to Miss Josephine then disappeared into the mirror.

CHAPTER TWENTY-FOUR

Pemba towed Amber through the tight market, glancing back occasionally and flashing her bright, big toothed smile. This was worse than the biggest sale at the mall, even Black Friday. People jostled against each other as they crowded the stalls to haggle for whatever they needed, but it was a friendly chaos with jovial banter and playful insults filling the stifling air.

"Here! This is the Mama Alla's stall!" Pemba announced. "She has the best dresses in Timbuktu!"

Amber forced a grin as she and Pemba arrived at Mama Alla's stall. Two brown mannequins posed on opposite sides of the stall, draped in the colorful dresses that most Timbuktu women wore. More dresses were stacked on the counter before them, some contemporary but most local. Behind it all was Mama Alla. She sat tall on a small stool, her aged face regal in appearance. Her yellow eyes focused on the fabrics in her hands, a new dress under construction. The dress she wore was a simple wrap of white, tainted by the constant dust of Timbuktu. She reminded Amber of Grandma.

"Hello Mama Alla!" Pemba shouted.

Mama Alla grinned but did not look their way. "Pemba, you're late."

Pemba looked back at Amber. "I come here every day. Her dresses are so beautiful!"

"She wastes my time," Mama Alla added. "Pemba never buys anything. Who are you talking to?"

"My new friend, Amber. She's needs a dress."

Mama Alla placed her latest creation on her lap and looked fully upon Amber. A slight smile came to her face.

"You're American," she commented. "But I see Soninke in you. You are a daughter come home."

Mama Alla's words warmed her heart. Amber did feel a certain comfort in Timbuktu despite the heat and dust. At first, she attributed it to her ability to adapt to different situations like Paris and Dakar, but it was different in Timbuktu. Very different.

"Which dress do you like, Amber?" Pemba asked.

"No," Mama Alla said. "Not these dresses. I have a special dress for your friend."

Pemba's hands flew to her mouth to cover her squeal.

"What?" Amber asked.

Pemba didn't reply. Before Amber could ask again Mama Alla rose from her seat then ambled to the back of her stall, waving the girls to her. They followed her behind the stall.

"I sense you are a special woman, Amber," Mama Alla commented. "And a special woman needs a special dress."

Mama Alla went to a colorful pile of fabric, digging to the bottom. She extracted an old suitcase held together by a pair of stretch cables.

"Did you know that amber used to be considered a precious jewel in Timbuktu?

"No, I didn't," Amber replied.

"Not only is it a jewel, it contains medicinal powers as well."

Amber touched her necklace. If Mama Alla only knew, she thought. When she looked into the woman's eyes, her expression hinted she probably did.

"This is your dress, Amber," she said.

Amber was not impressed. Whatever was in the old luggage couldn't possibly be worth much.

"I need to see it," Amber asked.

"No, no," Mama Alla replied as she shook her finger. "You will see it when you wear it."

Amber folded her arms. "I'm not buying anything I haven't seen. There could be a brick or something in that suitcase."

"Amber, don't question Mama Alla's judgment!" Pemba scolded. "Her opinion on such things is well respected."

"It's okay, Pemba," Mama Alla said. "She's American."

Amber didn't know how to react to that statement, but she wasn't going to pay for a dress she'd never seen. It was then she realized she wouldn't buy anything. She didn't have any money.

Mama Alla extended the suitcase to Amber. "Take it home and try it on. If you don't like it bring it back. If you do we'll negotiate a price."

"Go ahead, take it," Pemba urged.

Amber took the suitcase. "Thank you, Mama Alla. I hope I'll like it."

Mama Alla returned to her seat and continued sewing her dress.

"I know you will daughter. I know."

Pemba grabbed her arm then dragged her through the crowd. They stopped abruptly when they ran headlong into the back of a man dressed in western clothes like Amber. Amber tumbled over Pemba as they crashed into the dust. The girls scrambled to their feet, more embarrassed than hurt.

Amber dusted her clothes.

"I'm so sorry," she said. "We…"

"Amber. It's me."

She looked up at the man. Bissau stood before her, a wide grin on his face.

"Bissau!"

Amber leaped at Bissau, throwing her arms about his neck. She felt his hands gingerly touch her waist and she smiled.

"I'm so glad you're alive!"

Bissau held her a moment longer then pushed her away at arm's length.

"I'm glad I'm alive, too."

"How did you find us?"

"Nana Josephine's house is full of surprises," he answered. "Where is nana Alake?"

Amber's mood turned somber. "She is resting. She was injured when we arrived. Bissau, Grandma says we are close to Marai."

"We are," Bissau replied. "I will take us there soon."

Amber felt a warm sensation in her belly. She smiled at Bissau then grabbed his arm.

"Come on. I'll take you to Grandma."

Bissau stopped her. "Who is this?"

His eyes were suspiciously studying Pemba.

"She's Pemba. She was helping my find a dress."

Pemba nodded to him shyly. "Hello, Bissau."

Bissau nodded back, his look still guarded.

Amber took his arm again and they hurried back to the doctor's home.

"Amber, you must be careful," Bissau warned. "Everyone who is friendly to you does not always have good intentions."

"You forget my gift," Amber replied. "I'd know long before you."

Bissau nodded, a thoughtful look on his face. "That is true. I will trust who you trust."

"Where is that woman trying to stop us?" Amber asked.

"I have lost her for now, but I'm sure she's still looking for us."

"How is it that she can change shapes?" Amber asked.

"It is her gift," Bissau replied.

Amber ceased walking. "That's all? It's her gift?"

Bissau looked puzzled. "Yes, that is it. There is nothing else to tell. It is her gift as it is yours to see into one's heart."

"There has to be more to it," Amber said.

Bissau touched her shoulder. "Some things have no explanation. They just are."

Amber was about to continue the argument but thought better of it. She was not at school in some debate class; she was in Timbuktu trying to save her Grandma.

When they arrived at the doctor's house Grandma stood at the door. A wide smile came to her as Amber and Bissau approached.

"You found us!"

Bissau knelt before Grandma and took her hand.

"Yes, Nana. Miss Josephine has a master mirror in her possession. I used it to find you."

"A master mirror?" Grandma's face went from joy to concern. "Baba must know of this. That mirror can be a blessing or a curse."

Bissau nodded in agreement. "We are not far from Marai. With camels we can make the journey in two weeks."

Amber's chest tensed. "Camels?"

Bissau nodded. Grandma gave her a reassuring smile.

"It is the best way to travel in the desert."

Amber's chest grew tighter. "Desert?"

Grandma patted her shoulder. "Yes. Marai is hidden in the desert."

Amber found a chair and sat hard. Images of the desert popped in her head; scorching sand, a brutal relentless heat, dry cracked lips, and buzzards circling, waiting for the last person to die.

Grandma looked into her worried face and chuckled.

"Traveling in the desert can be dangerous if you're not prepared and you don't know where you're going."

"I will arrange everything," Bissau said.

"And I will help!" Pemba volunteered. She looked at Bissau with a gleam in her eyes. Bissau smiled back politely.

His words didn't make her feel any better. Bissau was a boy, period. Grandma explained to her the rite of passage and how a boy became a man in Marai society much sooner than in America but she still couldn't fathom Bissau being responsible enough to take them across the desert. Even when she recounted everything he'd done to this point it was hard to imagine. But then she decided to let her new-found skills decide for her. She looked at Bissau, the lean, handsome boy standing confidently before her and let go all of her thoughts as she focused on his heart. She went deep inside him, seeking what her mind wouldn't let her accept. What she found startled her. The surprised apparently registered on her face.

"What is the matter?" Bissau asked.

"Nothing! I just remembered I haven't contacted my parents in a while. They must be worried sick."

"My goodness, we haven't!" Grandma said. "Where's the phone?"

"In my bag." Amber hurried into the doctor's office in search of her bag, thankful for a reason to distance herself from everyone. When she reached the bedroom she sat hard, dropping her head into her hands. She let the realization of her new revelation sink in.

Bissau was in love with her.

She didn't see that one coming. She raised her head and sighed. "Wow. Oh wow."

With everything else to deal with now there was this. She stood and slowly searched the room for her bag. So, Bissau loved her. So what? He hadn't said anything about it. As far as she knew he never would. But why wouldn't he? She'd never been in love, but she suspected if she was she would find a way to let the object of her feelings know. She laughed aloud; she would probably walk up to the lucky boy and tell him outright. That was her way. But Bissau didn't reveal a thing. His smile was pleasant but not joyful and his words to her were always respectful. He never complimented her looks nor did he try to touch her in any way. He didn't even hold her when she hugged him, at least not like he meant it.

She shook her head. She was thinking about it all wrong. Bissau wasn't a boy from Buckhead or Cascade Heights. He was a man from Marai raised with different rules and standards. She thought back to Grandma's stories, the tales she thought were made up but she now realized were very real. There were all types of things to consider before a man could approach a woman for her hand. She shook her head.

"Find you bag, Amber," she whispered. "First things first."

She found the bag a couple of minutes later beside her bed. She opened it then sighed. Her phone was not inside. She walked back into the main room.

"My phone is gone. "

Pemba grabbed her arm. "It must be somewhere inside. I'll help you find it."

Pemba dragged her into the doctor's office. She was chattering as soon as they were away from the others.

"Bissau is so handsome!"

Amber felt an unexpected flash of anger.

"I…guess…so," she stammered.

"I've never seen him in Timbuktu."

Amber's hands tightened into fists.

"He's not from here."

Pemba's eyes widened. "Where is he from?"

Amber spun on Pemba.

"Hey, I'm not interested in talking about Bissau right now, okay? I just want to find my phone and get out of here!"

Pemba shrank back, pain evident in her expressive eyes.

"I'm sorry," Amber said. "I'm just tired I guess."

A realization came to her and she smacked her forehead.

"I know why I can't find my phone! I left it in Dakar."

She collapsed in the doctor's chair. Pemba came to her then patted her shoulder.

"You should change," Pemba replied.

"I wish I could," Amber mused.

Pemba smiled. "I meant your clothes. You should change into the dress Mama Alla gave you."

"Oh yeah, right." Amber had forgotten the dress. She went to the bathroom. Bissau and Grandma's voices drifted down the narrow hallway and she smiled. Despite everything it was good to be together again. She entered the bathroom, undressed quickly then sponged off. The process calmed her somewhat. As she dressed she considered her reactions to Pemba's questions about Bissau. Could it be she was jealous? No, that couldn't possibly be it. She'd only known him briefly. She was just tired, hot and …homesick. That's was it. She wanted to go home. The excitement of an adventure was gone. At least they were almost to Marai. She'd choose this Sana then go home and never see Marai again.

The dress fit perfectly, the fabric ideal for the conditions. Amber held the head wrap in her hand, having no idea what to do with it. She looked at herself in the mirror for a moment then smiled. Mama Alla knew what she was talking about. She left the bathroom and then entered the room with Grandma and Bissau. Grandma smiled when she saw her; Bissau's eyes went wide, him mouth forming a circle.

"Now you're home," Grandma said. Bissau said nothing.

Pemba clapped her approval. "You look beautiful!"

"Thank you," she replied. Her eyes went to Bissau again. A slight smile came to his face then he looked away.

"Pemba, where does one buy camels?" he asked.

Pemba beamed. "Come, I will show you."

"I'll come, too," Amber said, a little too eager.

"No Amber. Stay with me," Grandma insisted.

Pemba grabbed Bissau's arm then dragged him from the house. Amber watched them leave, fighting the illogical roil of emotions in her head.

"Come sit by me," Grandma said. "I'll fix your head wrap."

Amber sat by Grandma then handed her the head wrap.

"I'm glad you're better Grandma," she said

Grandma began wrapping her hair. "You've handled this well, grand baby. I didn't know what to expect from you, but you have exceeded everything I could imagine."

Amber let her guard down. She closed her eyes and sighed.

"I'm not doing as well as you think," she replied.

"You're doing fine. We're almost home. Once you select the Sana we'll be on our way."

"That shape shifting woman," Amber said. "Was she actually trying to kill us?"

Grandma patted her back. "The position of Sana is a powerful and cherished role. But the Maraibu are a different folk than those we know. I believe she's been sent to delay our arrival, nothing more. If you don't select the Sana the elders will. Whoever is trying to prevent our arrival has influence among the elders. It is the elders who will select the next Sana should we not arrive in time. The elders don't have our discriminating ability."

"Don't baby me," Amber said. "This is more serious than you say."

"We'll be fine," Grandma said. "Don't you worry. Now let's talk about Bissau."

Amber stiffened. "What about him?"

"I see the way you look at him and how he looks at you. Remember the stories I told you?"

"Yes."

"Well, the marriage of a man and woman in Marai is a very involved process."

Amber jerked her head from Grandma's hands. "Wait a minute! Who's talking about marriage?"

"Calm down, baby girl," Grandma said. "I'm just trying to explain some things to you. Attraction between men and woman is natural, but serious relationships can be complex. No one is suggesting that you and Bissau would want to marry or even date, but it is a situation that might cause friction if it came to be. So, it's best you do a better job at keeping your emotions under control."

Amber was about to argue but the firm look in her Grandma's eyes told her the conversation was over.

"I will," was all she said.

Grandma smiled and hugged her. "Good. Now let's take a look."

Amber stood then faced Grandma, striking a model pose.

"Beautiful!" Grandma said.

Amber went to the room then looked in the mirror. She loved what she saw. She made a note to add head wraps to her wardrobe.

"It's wonderful," she said as she went back to Grandma. "You'll have to teach me."

"I will. Now let's sit here all hugged up until Bissau and Pemba return."

The two returned about an hour later. Bissau's face beamed as he walked up to them.

"Everything has been arranged. We'll set out in the morning. Once we get to Marai we will be safe."

"We visited Mama Alla's booth," Pemba added. "I told her how beautiful you looked in the dress."

"How much do we owe her?" Grandma said.

"Nothing," Pemba replied. "She said it's a special gift for a special girl." Pemba frowned. "She never gave me a dress!"

"I'll give you the money," Grandma said. "You can buy your own."

Pemba squealed. "Thank you!"

Grandma turned her attention back to Bissau.

"Once we arrive at Marai how will we enter?" Grandma asked. "Is the barrier still intact?"

Bissau nodded. "Master Jakada has provided me with the means to penetrate the Veil."

Grandma sighed. "It's been so long."

"Yes, it has," Bissau answered.

Pemba looked at them in a curious way.

"Don't ask," Amber advised.

Amber took a quick glance and Bissau then looked away. Things were getting more complicated than she imagined. But now they were on the last leg of this strange adventure, she hoped. It couldn't have come at a better time.

CHAPTER TWENTY-FIVE

Aisha soared, her white wings buoyed by the rising desert air. She drifted in wide lazy circles, scanning the sands below with keen gyrfalcon eyes. For days she took to the sky, searching for Amber and the others. It was all she had left. Bissau was cleverer than she imagined which made her even more interested in him. He'd managed to hide from her completely despite her talents. But eventually she would find them. It was only a matter of time. She would not accept failure.

She jerked, freezing in mid-air. Terror gripped her as she tried to flap her wings but the invisible force held her still. Her physical strength was limited in this form, but transforming meant plummeting to her death. So she struggled as best she could as the force pulled her down. Had Bissau acquired new powers, or was the boy stronger than he let on? She finally realized her actions were fruitless; whatever held her would have its way. She relaxed and allowed the force to guide her. After a few hours the terrain below became familiar. The fear that subsided earlier returned but this time it was not accompanied with struggle. A vanguard of towering dunes appeared before her and she knew what she feared was true. She was in Bagule's grip, which meant he was not happy with her efforts. But how did he manage to extend his powers beyond the Veil? Things had changed in Marai if he was able to do so without Jakada's notice. She had to be prepared.

She drifted through the dunes that were not there, the sensation of Jakada's power tickling her skin. The barrier was weaker than when she first left on her mission. The city appeared below her soon afterwards and the force released its grip. Bagule knew she would come to him. She had no other choice. She flew to the white tower rising over the western section of the city, to the highest balcony giving entrance to Bagule's sanctuary. She transformed on the balcony then entered. Bagule sat on his favorite stool, his hands absently strumming his kora. Light danced on the strings as he played a random tune, the song that apparently found Aisha and pulled her back to the city. Nieleni sat beside him, humming in time with his playing, her voice as beautiful as her face. Bagule ceased playing when Aisha cleared her throat.

"Your efforts have been less that successful," Bagule said.

"There have been obstacles," she replied.

"Bissau the apprentice," Nieleni sang.

Aisha's eyes narrowed. "Yes."

"Still, you have accomplished something." Bagule stopped playing and placed his kora on a silken pillow. He walked to his desk and picked up a pouch.

"I expected more from you, but I should have known better. You are only a shape shifter. Your skills are limited. Despite your shortcomings you have delayed Alake's return so you deserve something."

He tossed the pouch to Aisha. She caught it and frowned. By its weight in her palm she could tell it was not the amount he promised.

"Thank you," she managed to say. "So, is it over?"

Bagule cut a glance at Aisha that made her stiffen.

"The mourning period is almost complete. Alake and her granddaughter have not appeared to select the new Sana, so the elders are ready to convene. Although Alake and the girl are on their way, they will never make it to Marai on time."

"On their way? How do you know this?"

Bagule smiled. "There are ways to reach out beyond the Veil. I have found other means to delay them."

He sat on his stool, picked up his kora and began playing. The music was mesmerizing. Aisha became dizzy. She turned to walk to the balcony and stumbled.

"Let me help you." Nieleni stood by her side, steadying her. She led Aisha to the balcony.

"Thank you for your services," Nieleni said. "You should check your payment to make sure you're satisfied with the amount."

Aisha steadied herself. "I'm sure it's not enough."

She opened the pouch and was suddenly covered in gold dust. The particles swirled around her like a whirlwind, lifting her off her feet.

"Goodbye, Aisha," she heard Nieleni say. There was laughter in her voice.

Again, Aisha wastransported against her will, but this time she had no idea of her destination. She drifted within the golden cloud until she felt her feet sinking into sand. The gold cloud cleared, replaced by the view of endless desert. She was outside the city. She tried to transform into the gyrfalcon to determine where she was but could not. She tried again, this time a desert fox. Nothing.

"Damn you, Bagule! You've stolen my birthright!"

Aisha glared at the horizon a moment longer then headed east. Bagule took her shape shifting, but he could not steal her instincts. First, she would find water. Then she would plot her revenge.

CHAPTER TWENTY-SIX

Amber studied the camel, her face bunched into a frown. It was big, ugly and it smelled like burned collard greens.

"We're riding this?" she said.

Bissau flashed his calming smile. "It is not so bad. You'll enjoy it."

Amber turned to Grandma. "You sure we can't rent a truck or something?"

It was Grandma's turn to laugh. "A truck can't take us where we need to go."

Pemba looked on, clearly upset. She approached Bissau.

"Are you sure I can't go? You may need my help."

Bissau grasped her shoulder. "You have been a great help, sister. Only a few are allowed where we are headed."

Pemba tiptoed then kissed his cheek. "Have a safe journey, Bissau."

Bissau's sour expression broke Amber's tension. She finally laughed.

Bissau forced a smile. "Thank you…sister.

"I will." Pemba seemed to be waiting for something.

"She wants you to kiss her back," Amber said.

Bissau looked at Amber, a pleading look on his face. Amber enjoyed his discomfort.

"Well?" she said.

Bissau leaned over and kissed Pemba's cheek. She threw her arms around him, hugging him tight.

"Be well, sister," he managed to say.

Pemba kissed his cheek again then skipped away.

Bissau hurried to the camels. "I'll help you on your camel."

He took the camel's reins and pulled it down. Amber climbed on awkwardly then the camel stood. She gripped the reins tight. She didn't realize she would be so high!

Grandma and Bissau mounted their camels easily. Amber sat stiff, afraid to move. Bissau turned to look at her and smiled. He guided his camel to hers then took the reins.

"Hut, hut!" he shouted, and the camels strolled into the desert. So it was really happening, Amber thought. They were going to Marai.

She rocked side to side with the beasts' laconic rhythm but the trek was anything but relaxing. She was going to fall. All these miles and adventures and her life was going to end in the desert when she fell off her camel and broke her neck. The thought made her tighten her legs about the camel and gripped her reins more. She was too young to die, she decided.

The sun wasn't as bad as she'd imagined. It was definitely hot, but she experienced hotter days during summers in Atlanta. Still, she was soon thirsty and hungry. She almost whooped when a small stand of desert palms broke the horizon. The camels needed no guidance to the respite, their pace quickening at the site of the verdant spot. By the time they reached the oasis edge the camels were trotting and Amber was doing her best not to tumble from her camel's back.

Bissau was able to bring his camel to a stop before it reached the glimmering lake. He dismounted then raced to Amber's camel, grabbing the reins and turning the beast. It grunted and spat at him. Bissau dodged the wet projectile then forced the beast down. Amber jumped off with a smile.

"Thank you so much!" she exclaimed.

Grandma managed her camel alone. The three of them followed the beasts to the water. They sat under a large palm tree, spreading out their provisions before them.

"We have more than enough to take us to Marai," Bissau said. "There is another oasis between us and the city. It's smaller, but it had date palms."

"How do you know all this?" Amber asked. "I thought you couldn't leave the city."

"I saw it in Master Jakada's mirror," he said. "I studied the outside for many weeks before starting on my journey."

"I thought you were to bring us back through the mirrors."

"I was, but I thought it would be best to figure out another way just in case things went bad, and they have."

"It was smart of you to do so," Grandma commented. "My father chose well."

"Yes, he did."

Their heads jerked to the direction of the familiar voice. Aisha emerged from the palms, a smirk on her face. Bissau sprang to his feet then took a defensive stance.

"Sit down, boy," Aisha said. "I mean you no harm."

Bissau advanced toward Aisha, his intent clear on his face. Amber concentrated on the woman, looking deep with her skills.

"Stop, Bissau! She telling the truth."

"She has skills, Amber," Bissau warned. "She can confuse your talents."

"The girl speaks right," Aisha said. "I mean you no harm, if only for my own reasons."

Amber nodded. "I sense she is our ally, but she is not our friend."

Bissau folded his arms across his chest. "Why are you here?"

"I'm here…to help you," Aisha answered.

Bissau laughed. "See, I told you she was lying. Why would you help us?"

"Because she's been betrayed," Amber said. "Whoever sent you to stop us has turned on you."

"The girl is correct again." Aisha looked at her with narrow eyes. "You are very good. I see why Bagule fears you. His lies would glow like a fire in your sight."

"So why should we trust a traitor?" Bissau asked.

Aisha glared at the young man. "Because revenge can be just as effective as honor."

Grandma approached Amber, her face just as concerned as Bissau. "Are you sure, Amber?"

"I'm sure," Amber replied. "She is sincere."

"Then help us," Bissau said. "Change into a bird and find out how far we are from Marai."

Aisha's sure smile faded. "I can't."

"See, I told you she lies!" Bissau extracted his knife.

Amber gazed again with her gift. The truth still reverberated inside Aisha, but now it took on a deep blue shade.

"No Bissau, she still speaks the truth. But now it comes from pain."

Aisha slumped to the ground, hugging herself.

"Bagule took my gift!" she hissed. "I don't know how he did it, but he stole my birthright. Then he dumped me in the desert to die. That's why I'll help you."

The skepticism finally faded from Bissau's face.

"How did you make it this far?"

"I'm a desert child," she answered. "I know the ways of this land. Still it was not easy."

"You must be thirsty," he said.

Aisha smiled. "And hungry."

She stood and staggered to the lake then drank. Amber went to her, handing her bread and meat. Aisha pulled away from the lake, her face wet and relieved. She accepted the food with grace then ate with passion.

"We'll camp here overnight then set out for Marai in the morning," Grandma said. "Bissau, how far are we from the next oasis?"

"A week at least," he answered

"We must be wary," Aisha said. "Bagule has sent others after you. I don't know who they are or where they will strike."

"Others?" Amber's hands shook.

Aisha nodded. "He is still determined to be Sana, and I'm sure he's still trying to prevent your arrival. He has found some way to extend his power beyond the Veil."

Bissau raised his head, scanning the foliage. "I will check the area."

Aisha raised her hand. "There's no need. If someone was here they would have made themselves known by now. I think we're safe for the moment."

They set up camp, resting the remainder of the day. Camping was something Amber was never interested in but here she was sharing a tent with her Grandma in an oasis under the wide sky. She was nervous, exhilarated and afraid. Aisha was helping them now, but whoever hunted her in the shape-shifters stead might be more dangerous than the revenge filled former shape shifter. She watched Bissau as he moved about the camp. He set up the fire, warmed the rations they brought with them and then prepared tea, of all things. Aisha was helpful as well. She fashioned some type of trap then managed to catch a few fish from the lake. Bissau reluctantly shared his knife with her and in moments they had fresh, tasty fish with their evening meal. The tension and exertions of the day finally took their toll on Amber. As the sun descended below the dunes she was ready to sleep.

"We must set up a watch," Bissau said. He looked at Amber with concern.

"I'll take the first watch," Grandma volunteered.

"No, nana, you must rest," Bissau said. "Amber and I will handle this."

As tired as she was she nodded her agreement.

"I'll help as well," Aisha said.

Bissau cut his eyes at her. He still did not trust her.

They all looked to Amber.

"Bissau will take the first watch," she decided. "I will take second. Aisha, you will take third watch."

Aisha grinned; Bissau's eyes narrowed as he looked at Aisha but nodded in agreement.

"Grandma, you rest," she said last. "I know this journey has been hard on you."

"I feel fine, Amber. As a matter of fact, I feel better than I have in quite some time."

Grandma did a quick step and spin to Amber's surprise.

"Don't overdo it," she warned. "I still have to take you back home to explain all this to Mama and Daddy."

Grandma laughed. "Now that's going to be interesting."

Amber, Grandma and Aisha bedded down as Bissau took first watch. Amber fell asleep immediately. It seemed she had just closedher eyes when Bissau shook her awake.

"I apologize Amber, but it's your watch."

Amber groaned as she sat up then covered her mouth embarrassed.

"I sound like an old woman."

Bissau smiled. "You sound like a tired woman. I know this has been arduous for you."

"It's been different, I'll admit."

The two looked at each other in silence. Amber looked away, remembering Grandma's words of advice. Now was not the time to go googly eyes over a boy.

"I can take your watch if you like," Bissau offered.

"No, I'll do it. I've been enough of a burden to you as it is."

"You are not a burden, Amber. You are the reason I am here. I'm proud Jakada chose me to find you and bring you home."

"Marai is not my home," she replied. "Grandma will be happy to see it, but I don't know what to expect."

"You will love it," Bissau replied. "I only wish you were visiting under better circumstances. It is not crowded and busy like your cities. The streets are wide and the people are friendly; well at least most of them. We do not have the machines that you have but we have nyama."

What is nyama?" she asked.

Bissau glanced away, a frown coming to his face. "It is hard to explain. It is like what you call magic but it is much deeper than that. It comes from the land and from the ancestors. They pass it on to us from the Most High. It is like Aisha says, a birthright. Everyone and everything possesses it and each person manifests it in their special way. Aisha's way is shape shifting; your way is truth seeing."

"And what is yours?" Amber asked.

"I am not sure yet. That is what Jakada is helping me discover."

"You are a brave man," she said. "Maybe that is your birthright."

"Bravery is not nyama," he replied.

"Maybe it is."

Amber absently reached out then touched Bissau's cheek with her fingertips. His skin was smooth and warm. She so wanted to kiss him, but not like Pemba. Bissau looked at her hand then ran his eyes along her arm to her face. His smile confirmed Grandma's suspicions. Amber drew her hand away.

"I'll take your shift. You must rest," he whispered.

Amber nodded. She went to Grandma then lay on her blanket, snuggling into her sandy spot. She lifted her head one more time before sleeping, looking toward Bissau. He looked away, settling into his shift. She lay back down and clinched her eyes shut. Keeping away from him was going to be hard.

CHAPTER TWENTY-SEVEN

It took a week to reach the second oasis as Bissau predicted. Amber's fascination with the journey had disappeared long ago. She was tired of being hot, tired of the monotonous food and tired of Aisha's incessant bragging. Apparently, her former enemy had decided they would be fast friends despite her previous attempts to hurt her. Grandma and Bissau paid close attention to the two, Grandma often smiling, Bissau scowling. He still did not trust the woman. Amber doubted he ever would.

This oasis was much larger than the first. To Amber it was truly paradise.

"Hut, hut," she shouted, urging her camel to a spirited trot.

"Amber, wait!" Bissau shouted. He started after her.

"Why?" Amber shouted back. "I can't wait to take a bath!"

Bissau was catching up to her when the jeeps burst from the palms speeding toward them. Aisha and Grandma joined them.

"Come, we must flee!" Aisha said.

"We can't outrun those," Amber replied. "Besides they might have guns. They would shoot us as soon as we tried to run."

"They would not shoot you," Bissau said. "You can run. We will stop them."

"Where would I go?" Amber asked. "I'm as good as dead here without you."

"What do we do?" he asked. There was an edge to his voice.

"We give ourselves up," Grandma said.

A sly grin came to Grandma's face. Bissau looked confused for a moment, and then he smiled as did Aisha.

Amber was still worried. She focused her skills on the approaching men and did not like what she sensed.

"These men are dangerous," she said. "Whatever you plan on doing you better do it quickly. I believe their intentions go beyond Bagule's orders."

Bissau looked at Aisha. "Are you up for this, shape shifter?"

Aisha opened her robe, revealing a dagger. "I am ready."

Amber's eyes went wide. The journey had become serious.

They rode together to the approaching jeeps. The men inside wore dingy turbans with scarves covering their faces except their eyes. The men carried AK-47 automatic rifles, though they were not pointed at the four for the moment. One of the men stood in the jeep.

"Which one of you is Amber?" His voice was deep and authoritative.

"I am." Amber's throat tightened as she answered.

"You will come with us."

Amber nodded. "What about my friends?"

"What about them?"

The men were lifting their guns when Aisha snatched out her dagger and flung it at the speaking man. He yelped then dropped his gun as the dagger plunged into his arm. Bissau leaped off his camel, landing in the midst of the men in the other jeep. Grandma guided her camel to Amber's mount then grabbed the reins. Together they galloped toward the cover of the oasis. Amber heard a shot then felt something hard and hot crease her head. The world tumbled before her eyes as pain blinded her like a bright light filling a dark room. Someone called her name from a distance but she couldn't make out who the voice belonged to. The light faded, and then there was darkness.

When she opened her eyes, her head throbbed. She lay on her back, her head propped on a rolled blanket. Amber reached up and touched the bandages. It was real. It did happen. Someone shot her.

"Baby?"

Grandma's voice was like a sweet song. She tried sitting up but her head hurt worse.

"Grandma?"

"I'm right here, baby." She felt Grandma stroke her hair and she smiled. A face appeared over her, one that was familiar and strange at the same time. She sat up, ignoring the dizziness and pain.

"Where are we?"

"Closer to Marai," Grandma answered.

"Amber!"

Bissau ran to them, a wide smile on his face. Aisha followed, her face contorted by her ever-present smirk. Bissau knelt beside her.

"You are better!" he exclaimed.

"Apparently," she answered as she returned his smile.

"You're a lucky one," Aisha said as she arrived. "A few inches to the right and this journey would be done. You can thank your bodyguard for that scratch."

Bissau glared at Aisha but said nothing.

"It's not Bissau's fault," Amber said.

"If you are to be a part of our team you need to learn how to support everyone here," Grandma said to Aisha.

"I won't take the blame for someone else's mistake," Aisha snapped. "If he was faster they wouldn't have fired one shot. My men were dead before he struck the first blow."

The word 'dead' hung in the air.

"Dead?" Amber said. "You killed them?"

Aisha's smirk faded. "I had to."

Amber eyes shifted to Bissau as her stomach churned.

"Did you kill the men you fought, too?"

"I did what I had to do to protect you Amber," he replied.

"No, he didn't kill them," Aisha answered softly. "I did."

So, this was not a game, Amber thought. People were dying to prevent her from reaching Marai. She wondered why it took her so long to realize how serious her journey was. Maybe it was because of the story Grandma told her long ago; maybe it was because of the travelling to different lands and Grandma's soothing words.

She looked around. In addition to the camels they now had a jeep, apparently taken from the men meant to kill her.

"How far are we from Marai?" she asked again.

"Not far, two days at least," Aisha answered.

Amber reached out to Grandma. "Help me."

Grandma helped her stand. She leaned against Grandma as dizziness came and went. The pain was still there, but she would handle it. She wanted to get to Marai as soon as possible. She didn't want anyone else to die, even if it was to keep her alive.

"I'm ready," she announced.

"Are you sure, baby girl?" Grandma asked.

"I'm sure. I'm ready to get this over with. I'm tired of being a target. I want to go home."

"We should rest another day to be sure," Bissau said. His words were more a statement than a suggestion.

"No, I want to go now," Amber replied.

"I don't think anyone else pursues us," Aisha said. "We are close to the city now. Bagule has no reason to send anyone else after you. Once you're in the city he can deal with you personally."

A chill raced through Amber. She looked at Aisha; the woman grinned back.

Bissau glowered at Aisha before speaking to Amber.

"Don't worry, Amber. Once you are in Marai you will be safe. You will be under the protection of Master Jakada. No one will dare challenge you. No one."

Amber wanted to believe Bissau but her senses told her otherwise. Uncertainty revealed itself in her young protector with a vibrant pink aura although his expression remained stoic and sure. Amber suspected his doubt arose from the incident with the bandits. Until that time he, and she, believed Bagule's power was contained within the city. They now knew that was not true. Aisha told them of the musical instrument which seemed to grant Bagule enhanced powers. He probably used it to breach her great grandfather's barrier. Amber's head throbbed again. She was speculating too much, but again her senses told her this line of thought was true. If that was so, they would have to be especially careful in Marai.

"Come on baby girl," her now sprightly Grandma said. "You need more rest."

Amber conceded. They spent one more day resting. At day break they broke camp and continued their journey. Grandma commandeered one of the bandits' jeep and Amber rode in the back, happy to have some semblance of the present. Bissau and Aisha rode their camels, leading the other camels packed with their provisions. They traveled the entire day at a slow but steady pace. Amber didn't feel like talking, which was rare for her. Her mind was more and more occupied with what lay ahead. She was mastering her skills, but could she actually accomplish what was required of her?

Her roundabout musing halted when Bissau stopped his camel then raised his hand. He came back to the jeep.

"We'll have to leave the vehicle here," he said.

Amber and Grandma abandoned the jeep then mounted their camels. They traveled another few miles then Bissau stopped them again.

"What's wrong?" Amber asked. A feeling answered her before Bissau, a sensation of calm and familiarity.

"We are here," Bissau confirmed.

Though her senses told her Bissau was right, her eyes registered nothing. All she could see was sand, scrub brush and dunes. Bissau dismounted his camel then approached Amber.

"You must take us inside," he said.

Amber felt a knot in her stomach. She looked at Grandma; Grandma smiled while nodding her head.

"He's right, Amber. The necklace is the key. It will work only for you."

"So, what do I do?" Amber asked.

"Lead us," Grandma replied.

Amber led the others toward the emptiness. At first, she didn't notice anything different but as she continued walking images began to form before her. Those images became definite shapes. The necklace warmed and the air before her shimmered. An acrid smell filled her nose and she stopped.

"What's wrong?" Bissau asked.

"Nothing," Amber replied. She took a deep breath then stepped into the wavering atmosphere. Her body tingled, the empty space pulling at her like gelatin against her skin. The barrier stung her eyes so she closed them, sure of her destination despite being unable to see. After a few minutes the prickling and pulling ended. Amber took a deep breath then opened her eyes.

Marai loomed before her, half hidden by a towering sandstone wall. Tips of towers peeked over the fortification, their white flags fluttering despite the slight breeze.

"I did it," she whispered. "I did it!"

She turned about then fear struck her. There was no one behind her. The barrier still simmered.

"Grandma? Bissau? Aisha?"

Maybe they're waiting for me, she thought. She walked back through the barrier, the tingling not as intimidating as before. When she reached the other side, dread replaced her fear. The camels were still there, but everyone else was gone.

"No, no, no!"

Amber ran through the barrier and into Marai through the open gates. Maybe they were ahead of her. The city was almost completely dark save for a few torches mounted on the walls of family compounds. She suddenly felt exposed, as if something or someone watched her from the narrow alleyways between the compounds. She ran from the middle of the street then took refuge in the nearest alley. There she waited, watching for the others to appear. After a few hours a frightening realization; she was alone. She slipped deeper into the alleyway, the darkness shrouding her from sight. Her hand went to her necklace. Its warmth comforted her, reminding her of Grandma's touch.

"Okay Amber, get a hold of yourself. The others are probably here. First thing to do is to find them. The next thing to do is to find great grandfather."

But what was she to do tonight?

She pulled her knees close then wrapped her arms around them. The stress of the day made her sleepy despite her situation and she yawned. There was no way she would even consider sleeping in an alley in Atlanta, but something told her that she would be safe in Marai, at least until the morning. She touched her necklace again and found reassurance in its warmth. She closed her eyes then fell immediately to sleep.

CHAPTER TWENTY-EIGHT

For the second time since her journey home Corliss was trapped. At least this time she was not unconscious in a cramped attic. A spacious room confined her within its walls, decorated with elegant rugs and silk sitting pillows. Bissau sat before her, his young face contorted in confusion. Aisha tugged at the door handle, grimacing with each effort. She finally stopped jerking the door handle then beat the ironwood door with her fists and feet.

"Let us out Bagule!" she shouted. "Let us out!"

Aisha's ranting informed her where she was trapped. Corliss could have told the fiery shape shifter to save her energy, but she had deeper concerns. Amber was not with them.

"Where is Amber?" Bissau asked.

Corliss shook her head. "I have no idea. Bagule must have known we would reach the city."

"So, he set a trap," Bissau said.

"But he didn't catch all the mice," Corliss replied. "I think the necklace protected her. Hopefully she was able to reach baba."

"What are you two talking about?" Aisha shouted. "We have to get out of here now!"

Aisha's outburst was answered by footsteps outside the door. They listened to jangling keys and then the squeal of the door handle as it turned. Aisha was poised to attack but her effort was deterred by three bodyguards entering the room with spears lowered. She back away with a snarl on her face. Bagule entered dressed in a billowing white shirt accented with golden threads. A simple white cape donned his head, a sneer distorting his ebony face. Nieleni accompanied him, resplendent in a flowing red and white dress and head wrap, her expression more reserved.

"Where is Amber?" he demanded.

"She is not here," Corliss said.

Bagule strode to Corliss then bent to face her.

"Don't toy with me Alake," he whispered.

His use of her little name made her jump. He knew more than he should.

"She did not come. Your attempt to kill her drove her away."

Bagule stood upright, worrying his chin. "So, she came this far and suddenly decided to go home?"

"She is a girl," Corliss replied. "It was too much for her."

Bagule strode by Bissau to Aisha. She glared at him then cut her eyes at the guards.

"Does she tell the truth, shape shifter?" he asked.

Aisha didn't answer.

"So, she lies." Bagule turned, striding back to Corliss. Bissau blocked his way.

"Stay away from her!" he warned.

One of the guards broke away from Aisha then rushed Bissau. The acolyte blocked his spear thrust then drove his foot into the man's gut. He doubled over, falling to his knees and then keeled over, striking his head on the floor.

Aisha sprang to her feet, knocking away the spears of the guards before her then rolling between them. She sprinted for the open door then ran into Nielini's fist. The woman then threw a studded orinka that crashed against Bissau's head, knocking him unconscious. Nieleni sat on Aisha, gripping her into a choke hold.

Bagule knelt beside Aisha.

"I'm very disappointed with you."

Aisha attempted to spit at him but Nieleni tightened her hold.

"I wonder if you would serve me again if I restored your abilities."

Aisha's face went slack and Bagule smiled.

"Yes, I can do it. But it comes with a price. First you will tell me if Amber entered the city, then you will find her."

"No, Aisha," Corliss whispered. "Don't."

"Your birthright will be yours again," Bagule said. "Will you serve me again?"

Aisha nodded her head. Nieleni let her go. Aisha fell onto her side gasping as she rubbed her neck.

"She...she walked through the barrier before us, but when we passed through we were here and she was not."

"How did she escape?" Bagule asked.

Aisha looked at Bagule. "I don't know."

Corliss felt some relief. At least she didn't tell him about the necklace. Maybe Aisha had her own plan to help Amber.

"Get my kora," Bagule said to Nieleni. The woman exited the room then returned with the instrument Aisha had described to them. Bagule cradled it like a child.

"Stand up, Aisha."

Aisha stood, her legs trembling. Bagule closed his eyes then plucked a complex tune. Aisha went rigid then collapsed. She lay still for minutes then stirred with a moan. When she finally looked up there was a smile on her face.

"The restoration is temporary," Bagule said. "You have two days to bring Amber to me. If you do not return with her in two days you will lose your powers permanently. Do you understand?"

Aisha nodded. "I understand."

Bagule's eyes narrowed. "You understand who?"

Aisha lowered her head, her shoulders slumped. "I under-stand...master."

Bagule smiled. "Good. Now go. You waste precious time."

The guards went to the window then opened it. Aisha hurried to it, climbed onto the window sill then looked back at Corliss.

"I'm sorry," she said. "This is who I am."

She leaped out the window.

Corliss dropped her head, despondent. Bissau still lay uncons-cious nearby. Without a mirror she couldn't contact baba and warn him of Bagule's intent. What happened to her was irrelevant. Amber was in danger and she had to find a way to warn her.

Bagule returned to her side. "So, what do we do with you, Alake?Don't worry. I am not a cruel man unless I'm forced to be. I will keep you here just in case what you say is true. With you locked away the elders will make the right choice. But if Amber is in the city then you are of no use to me."

Corliss didn't reply. She hoped Amber was safe. It was all she had left.

CHAPTER TWENTY-NINE

Amber awoke to insistent tugging on her left arm. She stretched before opening her eyes to the light of a rising sun. Something kept tugging at her arm; she looked down into the face of a goat.

"Eeek!"

The goat let go of her sleeve, bleated, then rejoined its herd passing the alley. The man shepherding them gave her a mean look as he passed.

Her joints were stiff and her stomach growled. She stood, stretched again then frowned as she sniffed her underarms. For a brief moment the seriousness of her predicament escaped her until the unfamiliar voices of Marai seeped into the alley. She tipped to the edge of the alley then poked out her head. The streets thrived with people. Women in long dresses and skirts similar to the one she wore but more brightly colored strolled with baskets fill with goods balanced on their heads while others carried gourds or held the hands of children tugging and pulling for freedom. The men wore loose fitting pants and large shirts rivaling the women's dresses in color. Some wore turbans, others cloth caps, while most went bare-headed despite the sun. Many carried goods and tools, while others herded goats through the throng. The crowd flowed in one general direction, toward the city center. With no idea where to begin looking for her great grandfather, Amber joined the crowd. Surely there was someone that could tell her where to find him. He was a great man in the city. Someone would know.

Marai reminded her of Timbuktu with its wide streets and mud brick compounds. The difference was the magnificent towers rising into the sky, each crowned with huge white flags signifying the end of the mourning period for the old Sana. Amber's stomach tightened. This was the reason she had come so far, to choose the next Sana. Despite everything she'd done and seen she still wasn't sure if she could do it.

She followed the crowd a few more yards before the people dispersed in every direction. Amber saw what she recognized as a market. Her senses were assailed by sights, smells and sounds both compelling and off putting; spices, the aroma of cooking foods, animals crying out over the voices of haggling people, and the stench of offal and death lingering in the background. The hunger in her stomach struggled with the nausea from the sight of slaughtered goats and others animals hanging before the butchers' stalls. She wondered if the goat that pulled at her shirt was somewhere dangling from a hook, its blood dripping onto the sand. The thought made her head spin and before she could gather herself she collapsed onto the ground.

"Make room, make room!" a woman shouted.

Amber felt her head lift. A smooth hand stroked her cheek.

"What is wrong, daughter?" the woman said.

"Grandma?" Amber asked.

"No daughter, I am not your grandmother." The woman sat her up. Amber looked into a kind sepia cherubic face graced with a gentle smile.

"Let's get you up, daughter," she said.

Amber struggled to stand. Another wave of nausea hit her and she slumped against the woman.

"When was the last time you ate, child?" she asked.

"Yesterday afternoon," Amber slurred.

"So that's it!"

The woman turned her head.

"Solonke!"

A girl appeared that seemed no older than Amber. She tilted her head, looking at Amber as if she was a strange bug.

"Who is she? What's wrong with her?" Solonke asked in an irritated tone.

"I don't know who she is," the woman replied. "I do know she's weak and she's hungry."

"Where is her husband?"

"You ask too many questions," the woman said. "Watch my stall. I'm taking her to our compound. She needs to eat."

"Why are you taking her there?" Solonke asked. "If someone is looking for her she'll be with you."

"Be quiet and do as I say!" the woman shouted.

Solonke frowned then trudged to the stall.

"Come, put your arm around my shoulder," the woman said.

Amber obeyed. Her head still woozy, she stumbled beside the kind woman into a walled compound near the market. She was suddenly surrounded by children, each of them struggling to get a look at her. One child, a boy wearing a red cap and a mischievous smile jumped in front of them.

"Who is this, Nana? What's wrong with her?"

The woman gently pushed him aside.

"Make room little ones," Nana said.

The children decided to help Nana, each one of them placing their handson Amber as if helping carry her to the nearest house. Nana took her inside then lay her down on a woven cot, placing her head gingerly on a padded head rest. She then handed Amber a gourd of water. It was lukewarm but refreshing nonetheless.

"Now daughter, tell me where you're from."

"I'm from..." Amber stopped. Where was she from? She had to be careful.

"Can I have something to eat?" she asked, stalling for time.

"Of course." Nana shuffled from the house. Amber took a long drink of water then looked around. Besides the bed there was a small stool and some sort of storage trunk. It was a sparse, especially compared to what she had at home. But there was no time for contemplation and comparison. She had to have a story about where she was from before Nana returned. After wracking her brain, she realized the only thing she could do was tell the truth.

Nana returned with a bowl of stew and a piece of flat bread that reminded Amber of a flour tortilla. She took the bowl and spoon then tasted the concoction. It was spicy, strange yet filling. She took two more gulps then cooled her mouth with the coarse bread and water.

"Now," Nana began, "tell me who you are and where you are from."

"My name is Amber. Jele Jakada is my great grandfather."

Nana looked at her strangely then frowned.

"I know you are weak Amber, but that does not give you the excuse for bad manners. I have taken you into my home and fed you. The least you can do is tell me the truth."

Amber was confused. "That is the truth, Nana. Jele Jakada is my great grandfather."

"Jele Jakada has no children," Nana replied. "His daughter died long ago and his wife died giving birth to the daughter, so there is no way you can be kin to him. I can tell by your clothes that you belong to a lineage family, but not Jele Jakada. Now let's try again, and please do not insult me any further."

Amber had no idea what to say. The truth didn't work and she didn't know enough about the city to make up any other story. Out of desperation she looked into Nana with her abilities, seeking something that would help her concoct a reasonable answer.

"You are hiding, aren't you?" Nana said.

"Hiding?" Amber decided to let Nana lead her to an answer.

"What would I be hiding, Nana?"

"You are marrying age," Nana said. "You are not the first woman to flee an arranged marriage."

Amber lowered her eyes as if what Nana said was true.

"Ah, I thought so!" Nana took her bowl then filled it with more stew.

"I bet you were promised to someone long before you were born. That is the way among those of lineage."

Amber remained quiet as she ate her stew.

"Running away will not solve your problem," Nana said. "When your family finds you, they will still insist you marry. But there is always a way out."

"That is why I must see Jele Jakada," Amber lied. "He can help me."

"He is a powerful man and well respected. When my husband returns I will ask him to take you to the city center. He may be able to get you an audience."

Amber smiled. She had no idea how to find the others, but if she could get to great grandfather maybe he could help.

"You lie down and rest now," Nana said. "I must get back to my stall. Solonke is lazy. She would give my merchandise away just to be done early. Such an insolent girl!"

"Thank you, Nana," she said sweetly.

"See, now this is how a daughter should be."

Nana left the room and went back to her duties. Amber lay back and managed to fall asleep. It seemed only moments passed before she was shaken. She swatted at the perpetrator.

"Go away, goat!" she mumbled.

"I am no goat, stupid girl!"

Amber sat up, rubbing her eyes. Her sight cleared to the angry face of Solonke.

"My mama helps you and all you have in return is insults."

"I'm sorry," Amber said. "I thought you were…"

"A goat," Solonke finished. "You thought I was a goat."

This was not going well. Amber sat up then smiled.

"I'm very grateful for your help."

"I would have called the constables," Solonke said. "Let them sort this out. Nana is always taking in strays."

This girl could be trouble. Amber considered taking her chances in the street.

"Maybe I should seek out the constables," Amber said.

"Don't be stupid," Solonke snapped.

"What's wrong with the constables?"

Solonke rolled her eyes. "Nothing is wrong with them. If Nana comes back and you're gone she'll punish me. You'll stay here until she gets back. After that I don't care what you do."

Solonke grabbed her wrists and looked at her hands. Amber snatched them away.

"What are you doing?"

Solonke smirked. "Looking at your hands. Not a callous on them. Rich girl hands. What are you really doing here? Your baba wouldn't buy you a new camel so you ran away? Decided to spend a day among the servants?"

Solonke stood, and then folded her arms across her chest.

"You should go home now and leave us alone."

"Solonke? What are you doing?"

Fear flashed across Solonke's face.

"Go home!" she snapped.

Solonke fled the room.

"Ow!" she cried out.

Nana entered the room frowning. She was followed by a man with ebony skin and a bright smile.

"Amber, this is my husband Amadou. He is a leather master and well known among those of lineage. He will help you reach Jele Jakada."

Amadou came closer to Amber.

"Who is your father?" he asked.

"I wish not to say," Amber replied. "I need to talk to Jele Jakada before I reveal my family."

"She doesn't have the best manners," Nana replied. "But she needs our help."

Amadou pinched his chin. "We will go to the Circle tomorrow morning. I have a delivery to make to the Diops. I will ask for Jele Jakada while we are there."

"Then it is settled," Nana said. "You will stay with us tonight. Solonke will attend to you."

"No, I will not!" Solonke shouted.

"Yes you will!" her father shouted back. "Disrespectful girl! It seems to be spreading." He gave Amber a long look before leaving the room.

Nana waited until Amadou was gone before speaking again.

"Don't pay attention to either of them," Nana said. "Amadou is stubborn and defiant and Solonke is his mirror. I think she will always remain in this compound because no man would marry such a woman."

"Maybe she doesn't want to marry yet," Amber said.

"That may be so, but that is not her choice," Nana said. "Some ambitious man will come along thinking he can change her. She is a beautiful woman despite her attitude. But he will find that the leopard does not change its spots."

Amber said nothing. She was not fond of this arranged marriage situation, but it was the perfect cover for her being somewhere she shouldn't.

Nana had a large family. A procession of daughters, sons, children and grandchildren filed into her room to see her. All were pleasantly curious except Solonke. She glared and insulted Amber whenever she appeared. Amber didn't know what she'd done to get on the girl's bad side. She was tempted to peek inside her emotions but thought better of it. The last thing she needed to do was tell this girl what was truly in her heart. Her issue might become physical and at this point Amber was not about to let anyone harm her.

The rest she was urged to get never occurred. That night, torches were lit to continue work in the compound. Solonke brought a strong-smelling lamp into Amber's room then dropped it on the nearby table.

"You will be gone tomorrow," Solonke said.

"Yes," Amber replied.

"Good."

Amber couldn't take it anymore.

"Why do you hate me? I have only been here one day."

"One day too long," Solonke snapped.

"I've done nothing to you."

"You are here. That is damage enough. Someone like you shows up and all I hear is how I should be more obedient, humbler, more everything."

"You are like your father," Amber said.

"How would you know?"

"Nana said so. Your parents criticize you, but that's what parents do. They think they are trying to help you, but sometimes their words hurt."

Solonke's sneer faded. She tilted her head as her hands fell from her hips.

"Is that why you ran away?" she asked.

Amber's eyes widened. She never considered coming to Marai running away but that's exactly what it was.

"Yes," she answered. "My parents give me everything except their time, which is what I want the most."

The two looked at each other for a moment in silent understanding.

"You should try to sleep," Solonke said. "It's a long walk to the Circle."

"I know," Amber lied.

Solonke's smirk returned. "No, I don't think you do."

Amber smiled back. "Thank you."

Amber attempted to sleep with no success. She was nervous about her journey the next day to meet her great grandfather, and she was anxious about the whereabouts of Grandma and the others. She sat up on her cot, listening to the sounds of the compounds; snoring, coughing, whispers and soft laughter. It was so much like home yet so different. She didn't know what Marai possessed that made it such a threat to the rest of the world, but she did know there were things beyond the Veil which could bring much comfort to the city.

Things she missed like air conditioning, ice, cable television and cell phones. She laughed; most of what she missed was things she didn't need. They were wants, plain and simple. She fell back on her cot then eventually succumbed to sleep.

CHAPTER THIRTY

Aisha flittered through the night, fighting the urge to fly into the flickering torches illuminating the streets of Marai. She cursed Bagule in every language she knew but it still wasn't enough. Her shape shifting powers had been returned, but not at full strength. She had to resort to lesser means to find Amber which hampered her search. Instead of soaring over the city as an owl or lurking the street as a cat, she was a moth. She struggled to the city streets, careful to not land where she would be smashed or crushed then transformed to her human form.

She was exhausted and it was too late to search for the girl now. Everyone would be secure in their compounds for the night. Aisha was certain Amber was in the city, but after some thought it made sense that she would not be with her great grandfather. She didn't know the way on her own. But then, where was she? Lost, most likely. Aisha spent the day searching alleyways, compounds and less savory areas of the city with no results. Someone had probably taken her in, but whom?

Aisha's stomach growled and she frowned. First things first, she thought. She took to the alleys, working her way to Central Market. There was always some merchant working late in preparation for the next day, and that merchant usually possessed something to eat. As she entered the craftsmen district she saw light leaking from one of the stone houses. Aisha knelt, grabbing a handful of dirt then rubbing it on her face. She tossed it generously about her clothes then took a pinch of goat dung to add a little aroma to her disguise. Her confident stride became a stumbling walk. She entered the shop noisily, falling to the floor then looking up at the weathered old man sitting before a loom with feigned shock.

"I'm so sorry uncle," she apologized. "I'm so sorry!"

The elderly man stood then squinted at her. He wore a fine pair of pants, a purple loose shirt and a cowrie studded cap on his bald head. A wealthy man despite his humble shop, she surmised. His children probably counted the days waiting for their inheritance.

"No beggars," the man said softly.

"I'm no beggar," Aisha said. "I'm only hungry for this night. All I ask is a bowl of sorghum and I'll be on my way."

"If I feed you tonight you'll be back tomorrow," the old man said.

"I won't," Aisha said. "I promise."

The old man shuffled away then returned with a bowl of cold sorghum. Aisha took the bowl, sat on the man's floor then began to eat.

"I thought you said you would go away," the man fussed.

"I'm going to want another bowl," Aisha said.

"You'll have to work for it," the man replied.

Aisha contemplated strangling the man to unconsciousness. She looked at his stern face then decided to play along.

"What do you wish me to do?" she asked.

"I have an order for ten rugs to deliver in the morning," he said.

Aisha sat the bowl down. "You want me to deliver the rugs?"

"No. I wouldn't trust you with that. You'll help me make them."

An emotion overtook Aisha, one she hadn't felt in a long time. Her eyes glistened as an old memory emerged from deep inside.

"I will help you," she whispered. She walked over to the loom then sat before it.

"You can weave?" the old man asked.

Aisha nodded. She ran her hand over the warp as memories of her father sitting before his loom captured her thoughts. He was a weaver, the best in Ghana, his carpets and clothing prized from the Joliba River to the Sahara.

"I will weave," she said. "You change the yarn in the shuttle as needed."

She began, quickly falling into a rhythm, the opening of the warp, passing the shuttle across with practiced speed.

"Slow down!" the old man puffed as he filled the shuttles with yarn.

"You want to be done by morning, don't you?

The old man nodded.

"Then keep up. I want more sorghum before then."

CHAPTER THIRTY-ONE

"Wake up, daughter. My husband is waiting."

Amber opened her eyes to Nana's smiling visage. Rubbing her eyes as she sat up, she accepted the bowl of sorghum given to her by Solonke. The girl winked then left the room.

Amber ate quickly, ignoring the strange taste of the local cereal. Nana nodded as she finished.

"You are better now. Amadou will take you to the central market."

Amber handed the bowl to Nana.

"Thank you, aunt," she said. "You have been most gracious."

A bright smile came to Nana's face.

"You've learned some manners!"

Amber smiled. There was a strict hierarchy among these folks and parents were highly respected. Amber imagined how much calmer her school would be if her classmates did the same.

Amadou entered the room.

"Come, we must go. It is a long journey."

"Will you come back today?" Nana asked.

"I hope so. It all depends on our guest," Amadou answered.

"Jele Jakada will be happy to see me," Amber answered.

"I hope so," Amadou said. His expression was not optimistic.

Amber grinned. "He will, uncle. I promise."

She was leaving the room when Solonke appeared.

"Here, this is for you." She stuck out her hand. In it was a leather band strung with beads the same color as Amber's necklace.

"When did you do this?" Amber asked. "Where did you get the beads?"

"I did it last night," Solonke replied. "Where I got the beads is my secret."

"Thank you," Amber said. She hugged Solonke tight.

"I hope you get what you want," Solonke said.

"I hope you do too," Amber replied.

The sun rested low on the horizon as Amber and Amadou left the compound, their destination the Central city. They traveled a wide avenue busy with citizens, some heading for the numerous markets and others carrying out their various crafts. Amber was amazed at how much time was spent on things she took for granted. Life in Marai was so different than home, or anywhere else she knew. The Maraibu lived in another time, cut off from the world because of her great grandfather's barrier. But why were they hidden? What was it that caused her great grandfather to do such a thing? It was the first question she would ask him when they finally met and things settled down.

"Amber!"

Amber jerked her head to the direction from where her name was shouted. Aisha ran toward her, a bolt of fabric balanced on her shoulder. An old man ran behind her, trying his best to keep up.

Amber was happy yet cautious. Aisha had helped her, but she also hunted her. Her necklace warming about her neck didn't help either.

"Aisha! Where are the others?"

"Bagule has trapped them," Aisha replied. She ran up to Amber then hugged her. Amber's arms stayed at her side.

"You know this girl?" Amadou said.

"Yes," Amber replied. "She came with me from…the Central City."

Aisha tossed the fabric bolt from her shoulder then pulled at her arm. The older weaver lifted onto his shoulder, a scowl on his face.

"Ungrateful goat!" he shouted as he hurried away.

Aisha ignored his insult. "Come Amber! We must rescue them now!"

Amber pulled back, her suspicion growing. "I think we should get my great grandfather's help."

"We don't have time!" Aisha came closer and Amber took a step back.

"Bagule restored my powers so I could find you. I tricked him into believing I would help him. Now that I have we must return to help the others. We don't have much time."

Amber took another step back. The necklace was practically glowing.

"You're lying," Amber said.

Amadou stood before Amber.

"I don't think this woman is your friend," he said.

"She's not," Amber agreed.

Aisha kicked Amadou's shin. The man winced then bent over; Aisha struck him across the chin with her fist and he crumpled to the ground. She glared at Amber.

"Why must you make things so…"

Amber kicked Aisha in the stomach then punched her hard in the face. Aisha fell back on her butt, her nose bleeding. Amber turned to run but was enveloped by a wall of sand and dust. The swirling particles separated into eight columns. Aisha jumped to her feet.

"Get behind me!" Aisha shouted.

"So now you're helping me?"

Aisha smiled. "Against these, yes. No one is taking my bounty!"

Amber didn't heed Aisha's words. Instead she stood back to back with Aisha, crouching low then raising her fists high like Grandma taught her long ago. The columns solidified into men wearing sand-hued robes, each with their faces covered. Four of the men held swords, the others rope.

"I never thought Bagule would go this far," Aisha whispered. "This is no game, Amber. Make every strike count!"

Aisha let out a scream then attacked. Amber stood frozen, caught between confidence and fear. Her necklace urged her forward, but her emotions kept her in check. Something bumped the back of her leg and she looked down. One of the men lay unconscious, his eyes bruised. Aisha was a whirlwind of punches, blocks and kicks surrounded by her determined attackers. A rope fell over Amber; she tossed it away before the second rope reached her. The rope throwers lunged at her but she rolled between them, coming to her feet before another man with his arms outstretched.

Instinct took over. Her foot flashed between his legs then her fist crashed against his jaw as he crouched in pain. She slipped away from another man, kicking his feet from under him. Arms grabbed her then held her tight; she threw her head back, smashing it into her captor's face. The pain almost made her black out but the man lost his grip and let her free.

"It's too many!" Aisha shouted. She kicked another man in the shins then ran at Amber.

"Grab my hand!" she shouted.

Amber tripped up another man as she dodged his rope.

"What?"

"Grab my hand!"

Amber met Aisha then they joined hands. The world twisted then she was looking down on the gathering crowd.

"Follow me," Aisha said.

Amber looked in the direction of Aisha's voice and saw some kind of hawk.

"Follow me!" the hawk said.

"Aisha? You're a hawk!"

"You are too," Aisha replied. "I didn't think I could do it, but that necklace of yours helped."

Amber looked at herself. There were wings beating where her arms should have been.

"This is not real," she whispered.

"Come on," Aisha insisted.

"Where are we going?" Amber asked.

"To Bagule's compound!" Aisha said.

Together they flew toward the Central City, soaring over the mud brick compounds to a tower looming over an expansive compound. They settled on an iron railing outside a large shuttered window.

Aisha jumped off the railing, transforming as she landed on the balcony. Amber looked at her astonished then felt herself falling backwards.

Aisha grabbed her flailing hand then pulled her onto the balcony. Amber tumbled into her then both of them rolled into the room.

Grandma sat in the corner of the room, Bissau's head cradled in her lap.

"Grandma!"

Grandma looked up and a wide smile broke across her face.

"Amber!"

Bissau stirred, his eyes opening to slits.

"Amber?"

He struggled to sit up as Amber ran to them then hugged them both. She turned to see Aisha walking toward the door.

"Where are you going?" Amber asked.

Aisha grinned. "To claim my reward."

Amber thrust out her hands like she did in the restroom at the pizza joint. Aisha lifted from her feet then slammed into the wall. Amber kept her hands extended, pinning her to the wall.

Aisha glared at her. "You don't know who you're dealing with!"

Amber glared back. "I think I do."

She released Aisha as she reached her. No sooner did Aisha's feet touch the ground did Amber deliver a right cross that sent Aisha to the floor unconscious.

Grandma and Bissau looked at her, their mouths open wide as she strode back to them.

"How are you, Bissau?" she asked.

Bissau stood. He swayed a little. Amber grasped his shoulders to steady him.

"I feel good," he said.

"Good enough to fight?" Amber asked.

Bissau nodded.

Amber looked at her Grandma. Her face seemed less wrinkled, her eyes bright and expectant.

"I am ready too," Grandma said.

Amber went to the door.

"No," Grandma said. "You are coming into your own, but you are not strong enough to confront Bagule."

"Bagule is not here," Amber said.

"How do you know this?" Bissau asked.

"I'm not sure," she answered. "I just…feel like he's not here."

"Don't just feel it, Amber," Grandma said. "Be sure."

Amber closed her eyes, concentrating on the compound.

"There are four people on the other side of this door. Bagule is not one of them."

"Nieleni may be," Bissau said.

"Who is that?" Amber asked.

"Don't worry," Grandma said. "I'll handle her."

Grandma strode to the door then banged on it with her fist.

"Help us! Help us!"

She stepped away as keys jangled around the lock. As the door opened Grandma grabbed the hands of the key holder, jerking him into the room. She twisted, throwing him hard to the floor.

Bissau met the second man, deflecting his spear thrust with his wrist then delivering a swift combination of punches and kicks that sent the man reeling to the floor.

The third man and fourth man charged in swinging their swords. Amber pressed against the wall then stuck out her foot, tripping the first one through. The second man turned toward her then swung his blade. Amber ducked, the blade cutting into the wall as she drove her fist into her attacker's stomach. She rose on the balls of her feet as she delivered an uppercut to the man's falling chin. Bissau followed him to the floor, striking him hard on the temple to make sure he didn't rise again.

"Let's go!" Amber shouted. "Bissau, lead the way."

Bissau nodded then went into the next room. Nieleni stood in the center of the room, her arms folded across her chest, a scowl on her face.

"I didn't sense her!" Amber said before flying into the wall. She blacked out for a moment; when she opened her eyes Grandma and Bissau were fighting the skilled woman. The necklace warmed against her skin and she knew what to do.

She thrust out her hands and Nieleni stumbled. Nieleni's head jerked toward Amber.

"You!" she shouted. Nieleni raised her glowing hands. She clapped them together just as Grandma jumped before her. Amber screamed as blinding light engulfed Grandma. She fell to the floor, smoke rising from her body.

Amber crossed the distance between her Nieleni with amazing speed, punching the woman with all her might. Nieleni staggered backwards across the room then slammed into the wall. Amber was upon her before she could stand, kicking the woman in the face. Someone pulled her away after the third kick.

"Amber no." It was Bissau's voice. Amber kept kicking at Nieleni, tears running down her face.

"Stop Amber! Alake is not dead!"

Amber jerked about to see Grandma stirring. She broke away from Bissau then ran to her.

She helped Grandma sit up. Grandma shook her head then shared a weak smile with Amber.

"I'm okay," she said. "We must leave before they awaken."

"Are you strong enough?" Amber asked.

"I have to be."

The trio crept through Bagule's house then into the compound. Bissau led the way, his eyes darting back and forth as they ran across the open courtyard. They were almost to the gate when sand began swirling around them.

"Not again!" Amber said.

"I know how to deal with them," Bissau said. He reached into his pocket, extracting a handful of powder. He flung the powder into the sand as the assassins took shape then stepped away. When they finally materialized they were frozen like statues, surprised looks on their faces.

Bissau kept running. Amber and Grandma followed, Amber stumbling as she glanced back at Bissau's work. She turned away then caught up Grandma and Bissau as they melded into the street traffic.

Bissau pointed at a distant tower flying a red and white flag.

"That is Jele Jakada's tower," he said. "We will be safe there."

Amber shuddered. She grabbed Bissau to keep from falling. He grasped her tight.

"Amber?"

"Feeling weak," she managed to say.

"She did too much," Grandma said. "I'll get a cart."

Amber's legs gave way and Bissau lowered her to the ground. A crowd gathered around them.

"Don't worry," Bissau said. "You're safe. I promise."

Amber smiled. "I know."

She passed out.

CHAPTER THIRTY-TWO

Amber awoke exhausted and famished. Grandma loomed over her, her comforting smile lessening Amber's fatigue but not her hunger.

"I could eat a horse," she croaked.

"I don't have a horse, but I do have dates."

Grandma handed her a plate of the desert fruit. Amber remembered not being particularly fond of them, but at that moment they were the best fruit she'd ever tasted. Her hunger dulled immediately; she set the plate down and sat up. Lush pillows and chairs encircled her, the smell of pleasant incense calming and comforting. Bissau slept on a bed opposite, his head propped on a gilded headrest. But it was Grandma who intrigued her the most. She was no longer the elderly but sprightly women she'd set out on this journey with. She was much younger, resembling the old photos she'd seen in the house.

"Yes, I've changed somewhat," she said, answering Amber's questioning eyes.

"But how?"

Grandma chuckled. "Marai is selfish with her time. She takes back what belongs to her."

Amber didn't understand Grandma's words.

"What are we going to tell mama and dad?"

Grandma looked thoughtful. "That's a good question. We'll figure that out when we see them again. In the meantime, it's time for you to meet my baba."

Amber ate another date. Energy eased into her body with each fruit. By the time she finished she felt refreshed.

"I think I'm ready," she said.

Grandma led Amber to adjacent room. It was simply furnished; a small desk with a cushioned stool and a plain chest of drawers close by. The most prominent item was a large mirror bordered by a frame obviously carved by a true artist. The patterns of stylized animals and people captivated Amber so much that she almost forgot the reason she'd come to the bedchamber.

"Amber, meet my baba Jakada," Grandma said.

She broke her gaze from the mirror then looked to the opposite wall. Grandma's baba lay on a simple bed, his head supported by a plain head rest. His white robes fell over the edge of the narrow bed, his chest rising and falling slowly. He shifted then turned toward them both. A weak smile came to his bearded face.

Grandma went to his side and then sat beside the bed. Amber approached then stood beside her.

"You are here at last," he said. "Marai is safe."

"Hello, baba," Amber said.

"Your voice sings like Alake's when she was your age," he said. His eyes strayed to Grandma.

"It feels strange seeing you as an elder," he commented. "Though I saw you in the mirror this way, to see you before me is much different. You were still a child when I let you go."

Grandma smiled. "You will meet my family one day. I promise. I am sorry you never met my husband."

"I am, too." Great grandfather touched Grandma's hand.

"But there will be time for such meetings, I hope," he said, his voice becoming stern. "Bagule still hopes to be selected Sana of Marai. He knows you escaped and has stationed his allies around the elders' chamber to prevent you from entering. You must get inside."

"But how?" Amber asked. "I'm assuming his 'allies' are warriors."

Baba nodded. "They are. But you are not alone and you have your own skills."

Amber shivered. Her skills were not certain and appeared on their own accord. Bissau entered the room. Aisha followed with a sly grin on her face.

Baba grinned. "Ah, our wrestlers have come."

"What is she doing here?" Amber said. "She's with Bagule!"

"I'm with whoever pays," Aisha replied. "Jele Jakada has restored my abilities so I owe him a debt. Besides, you impress me. I'd like to see how this all works out."

Amber looked to Grandma. "Do you trust her?"

"She's a woman of her word," Grandma said. "We need her help as well. There are not many who will stand against Bagule."

"There are others that will assist us," Baba answered. "It's best they remain concealed until they are needed. What happens today will determine not only the fate of Marai, but possibly your world, too."

"What is happening, Baba?" Amber asked.

Great grandfather sat up. He seemed to be getting stronger as they spoke.

"Marai is an old city, older than you can imagine. It is the center of all things good and wonderful, but it is also the center of all things dark and dangerous. Our ancestors realized this early in the city's existence and decided in their wisdom to seal the city off from the rest of the world. A spell was created to do so, one that would render Marai invisible to all."

"But what about the people of Marai?" Amber asked. "They have done nothing! This is like a prison." She thought about Solonke and the kindness of her family.

Great grandfather nodded. "Some would think so, especially Bagule. It seems we are being punished for a condition we did not ask for. That is not the issue. The reality is that we have been given a great responsibility and we owe it to our ancestors and the rest of the world to be diligent of it."

"Still, I can understand why Bagule feels the way he does," Amber admitted.

"How can you say such a thing after what he's tried to do to you?" Bissau said.

"Because she is who she is," Grandma answered. "And she wears the necklace."

Amber touched the necklace around her neck. She'd worn it nearly all her life, never imagining its power. Now, sitting before Grandma's baba and the others the responsibility rested on her shoulders.

"So, what will we do?" Amber asked.

"My friends will come for you tonight," Great grandfather said. "They will take you to the Elders' chamber where the deliberations are being held. You will go as servants bearing refreshments. We have someone inside who is awaiting your visit. Once you get inside you will go to the kitchens and replace the servers. When you are in the presence of the Elders you will reveal yourselves."

"But how will they know who I am?" Amber asked. "And why will they believe me?"

"You must figure that part out," Great grandfather replied. "I have faith you will."

It was not a good plan, Amber thought. Her secret would be out and she would be exposed to anyone who meant to do her harm.

"And if I can't convince them?"

"Then I will get you out of Marai. You are only a threat to Ba-gule as long as you are here. If you are gone, he will leave you be."

Amber looked into her great grandfather's eyes and saw the lie. Bagule's reach extended beyond Marai's walls.

"What about you?" Grandma asked. "If Bagule becomes Sana you will not be safe."

Her great grandfather grinned. "Then I will finally learn what life beyond Marai is like."

Another lie, Amber sensed. He would never leave Marai. He would die first.

She glanced at the curtains. Night was coming, the waning light fading behind the colorful fabric. A few weeks ago, she was an awkward girl struggling her way through middle school. Now she was sitting in a city that shouldn't exist making a decision that she was not qualified to make. It was like being in a movie she didn't ask to be in, or having a dream she would rather not have.

Her great grandfather touched her hand and broke her thoughts.

"I know this is much for you to comprehend, but you have performed well beyond my expectations," he said. "That alone tells me that you can do this. Once the selection has been made you can return to your home and your life. The Sana of Marai is a long-lived person. You will never have to see this city again."

She'd never considered that. How was she going to forget this? And did she want to?

"Let's get some rest," Grandma said. "We have a long night ahead."

She followed Grandma back to her room then lay down on a hard bed with a plush silk head rest. Amber slept soundly, dreaming of home, mama and daddy. When Bissau shook her awake she was well rested.

"Amber, it is time."

Amber sat up on the edge of the bed then took a deep breath to calm the tempest in her stomach. This was it. In moments she would stand before a council of men and women to make a decision that would change the course of their lives. She shut her eyes tight, trying to imagine the scene, attempting to convince herself she was ready for this.

"Come now," Bissau urged. "We must go."

She took another deep breath then stood, pushing out her chest as she straightened her back. She strode into her great grandfather's room projecting more confidence outside than she possessed inside. Grandma, Bissau and Aisha stood by great grandfather's bed, joined by three people she did not recognize. Two men flanked a woman who wore as flowing head wrap and large golden earrings. She gave Amber a motherly smile before coming to her and taking her hand.

"I can feel it," the woman said. "She is definitely the one."

"This is Baramouso Sissoko," great grandfather said. "She is a trusted friend. She will take you to the elders' council."

Grandma bowed to Baramouso and Amber did the same. The woman waved her hand with a smile.

"Come, we must hurry," she said.

The two men accompanying her lit their torches then led the way with Bissau and Aisha close behind. They entered the dark dusty streets, walking swiftly up the wide avenues. As they approached the main market Amber felt a chill course through her.

"Wait," she said.

Grandma came close to her.

"What is it?" she asked.

The chill increased.

"Something is coming!" Amber exclaimed.

Baramouso's eyes widened.

"Everyone back!" she barked.

They ran back then hid in the nearest alley. The chill Amber felt transformed into a concoction of fear, disgust and anger. She looked at Baramouso, who confirmed Amber's feelings with a curt nod.

"A jinni approaches," Baramouso whispered. "It was probably summoned by Bagule. It is good you sensed it."

The jinni appeared in the road, an apparition resembling a sentient cloud with red orbs that searched about like eyes.

"I think I can stop it," Amber whispered back.

"No," Baramouso said. "I don't doubt that you can daughter, but now is not the time for you to reveal your skills. If the jinni does not report back to Bagule he will suspect something. We hide until we are close. Then all will be revealed."

Amber looked at Grandma and she nodded her agreement. They waited for the grim being to pass before continuing.

"This way," Baramouso said with a wave of her hand. "Hurry!"

They worked their way stop and go through the city, dodging more jinni.

"Why do they not see us?" Amber asked Baramouso.

"The jinni doesn't possess long range sight or hearing. Touch is the way of identity for these ones. Most don't recognize the jinni as they are. They think they are patches of fog or smoke. But you have the gift. Others are not so lucky."

They finally reached the center of the city, the home of the Sana. The tall walls resembled those of the private compounds but were constructed of huge blocks of granite. A wide gate occupied the center of the wall, rising several feet higher than the wall and dwarfing the guards patrolling either side of the entrance. The gate was open, its towering ironwood doors turned inward.

"Now we play our role," Baramouso said.

Amber reached out to the men at the gate. They were diligent and suspicious, as guards should be.

"They will question us," she said.

Baramouso smiled. "I know, which is why I will do all the talking. Keep your eyes down and say nothing, especially you, Amber."

Amber nodded then pulled her hood over her head. The group stepped out into the open then marched single file to the gate, Baramouso leading them. The guards straightened then stood before the entrance, crossing their spears between them then resting their free hands on the hilts of their swords.

"Good evening, sons!" Baramouso called out. "I hope we're not too late!"

"Mama Baramouso," the guard on the left said. "What are you doing here?"

"The elders sent a message that they needed more servants so I brought them," she answered.

"There have been no messengers," the other guard said.

Amber tensed. Aisha began to step from the line; Amber grabbed the back of her robe.

"Let me go," Aisha whispered. "I'll deal with them."

"No," Amber answered. "Let Baramouso handle this. They are trained warriors."

"So am I," Aisha replied. "This will be easy."

"Quiet!" Baramouso shouted at them in a commanding tone.

Aisha allowed Amber to pull her back in place.

"I'll give her a few more minutes," Aisha whispered.

Baramouso turned her attention back to the guards, a smile on her face.

"It's so hard to get good servants these days. Now, where were we?"

"There have been no messengers," the guard said, his voice more forceful.

"You actually think the elders would send me word through a mere messenger?"

The guards glanced at each other then stepped aside. Baramouso walked through the door. As Amber approached the curious guard stopped her then began lifting her hood.

"What are you doing?" Baramouso asked.

"Inspecting your servants," the guard replied.

"That is not necessary," she replied.

The guard turned to her. "I'll determine what's necessary."

"This is rude behavior, Diallo," Baramouso scolded. "You treat my assurance like dust. I know your mother raised a better warrior than this."

Diallo held the edge of Amber's hood between his fingers. He glared at Baramouso, apparently angered by her words. He snatched his hand from Amber's hood.

"Go!"

"Now that is the courtesy I'm used to," Baramouso said.

Amber and the others followed Baramouso down the corridor leading to the elders' chamber. More guards lined the walls and stood before the chamber entrance, their eyes on the group. Baramouso waved everyone to her.

"We will proceed directly to the meeting hall," she said. "Do not stop for anything or anyone. We will run if we have to. The main task is to get Amber before the elders. Nothing must stop us from doing so. Are you ready?"

Everyone nodded. Amber felt someone touch her hand and smiled.

"Don't worry," Bissau said. "I will protect you."

"I don't need your protection," she answered. "But I'm glad you'll be with me."

They hurried down the corridor, ignoring the curious stares and questions from the other guards. They were halfway to the hall when the questions became shouts. Amber turned to look behind her. A group of warriors and others were running after them, including the guards at the compound gate.

"Run!" Baramouso shouted.

Bissau let go of her hand then ran in the opposite direction. He joined Aisha at the end to their line, apparently preparing to defend her if the warriors caught up with them. Grandma pushed her ahead.

"Go, Amber! You must make it to the hall!"

Amber ran, following Baramouso to the chamber. The woman was surprisingly fast despite her age, as was Grandma. But Amber knew Grandma was changing, growing younger the longer they were in Marai.

The door guards took defensive positions before the chamber entrance, their weapons drawn. A hand gripped Amber's wrist then yanked her back.

"Get behind me!" Grandma shouted.

Grandma bounded straight into the warriors. They apparently didn't expect her to attack. Grandma delivered a quick kick to the first warrior's stomach then a palm heel strike to his jaw as he doubled over. The man hit the floor unconscious as the other warrior moved to attack her. She stepped into the second warrior's swinging arm, delivering a twisting elbow to his head. He fell away gripping his broken jaw. The third guard approached slowly with his sword and shield. Grandma took up the unconscious warrior's weapons then they circled each other. They clashed as three more guards appeared from inside the chamber.

Amber turned to call Bissau but he didn't respond. He and Aisha battled the warriors that came down the hall, Bissau fighting with quiet determination, Aisha yelling like a bad martial arts movie. Baramouso and her companions also fought, which meant there was no one to stop the three warriors coming at her. They brandished no weapons; their intent clear. They meant to capture her.

Amber remained motionless as the first man advanced on her. As he reached for her she grabbed his wrist then twisted, snatching the shocked man off his feet then throwing him. She continued to spin, crouching low then extending her left leg, sweeping the next man off his feet. As he crashed to the floor Amber rose, jumping over him as she delivered a snap kick to the third man's groin. He crumbled to his knees, his hands instinctively groping his privates. She let her momentum take her over him, landing gently on the balls of her feet.

"Amber!"

She looked in the direction of the call. Grandma and Baramouso pulled at the chamber doors, Grandma motioning her with her head. Amber wanted to stay and help her friends, but this was the reason they'd come so far. As the door opened she sprinted inside the elders' chamber. There was a collective gasp from those inside as she entered. She quickly surveyed the scene. The elders sat in a circle, each resplendent in their colorful robes and jewelry. Guards were spaced evenly against the wall of the circular room, each brandishing a sword and glaring in her direction. In the center of the circle stood Bagule, Nieleni by his side in a beautiful silk dress, her face still bruised from their earlier encounter. She glared at Amber, but Bagule seemed amused, a knowing smirk on his face.

"And so, she enters," he said, gesturing toward her with his free hand. The other hand held the kora.

"Elders, I present to you the great granddaughter of Jakada, the woman from beyond the Veil, Amber."

Amber straightened, her skills focused on the crafty noble. He hadn't been able to stop her from coming to the council, so he would attempt to discredit her. Grandma and Baramouso joined her, Grandma on her left, Baramouso on her right.

"Jakada convinced us centuries ago that we must separate ourselves from the world, less it taints us and we it. We agreed, allowing him to use his powers to hide us from its contamination. Yet standing before you is proof that Jakada's words pertain only to others but not to himself. How long has it been since anyone has seen his daughter Alake? Well here she is elders, standing before you as a young woman with not only a child of her own but a grandchild. If she was among us she would be no older than her grandchild. Our humble protector has separated us from the world while he uses the Veil as he chooses."

"My father sent me away to save me," Grandma said. "He knew the day to choose a new Sana was drawing near and he knew there were some that would not want the new Sana to be chosen the old way. He could not protect me in Marai, so he allowed me to escape."

One of the elders, a thin man with a wisp of a beard, cleared his throat.

"Who would wish to harm you, child? We are all brothers and sisters under the ancestors' watch."

Grandma cut her eyes at Bagule. "Some of you would choose a Sana not based on who you think would be best to rule Marai, but by whom you think would best serve your interests."

The elders shifted uncomfortably. Bagule's face became angry.

"How dare you insult the integrity of our elders!" he shouted.

"And how dare you attempt to buy them like cheap cloth!" Grandma shouted back. She grasped Amber's shoulders. Amber tensed with her touch.

"This is what we came for, Amber," she whispered. "You must be strong and open your mind to your powers."

"My granddaughter possesses what I have lost to time," Grandma said. "She will choose the next Sana."

Bagule laughed. "Are we to trust the seed of Jakada, the very man who trapped us here? The man who has violated his own edicts to satisfy his whims?"

"Then let me judge you," Amber said. The words surprised her as much as they surprised everyone in the room.

"Yes, let her judge you," Grandma repeated.

A stout woman with huge golden earrings and a collection of necklaces stacked from her shoulders to her chin raised her hand.

"Why would you judge us? We are not candidates."

Grandma leaned closer to her.

"That is Yenge Diabate, highest elder. Her family is the oldest lineage of Marai and the most powerful. Address her as Nana."

Amber stepped away from Grandma's grasp then bowed deeply.

"Nana, my talent allows me to see into your heart," she said. "There are no secrets to me. Give me your hands. I will share only with you something that no one else knows, not even your husband. If I can do so, then surely I can select the new Sana."

Yenge approached Amber, her hands extended.

"Show me," she said.

Amber took Yenge's hands. She closed her eyes then cleared her mind. Images swirled into the emptiness, forming shapes and symbols she couldn't comprehend. She let go of Yenge's hands.

Bagule looked into her eyes, a triumphant smile gracing his face.

"See? This is a waste of time."

"Let me try again," Amber said. "I'm not from here. The symbols are different."

Yenge gave Amber her hands again.

"Try again, daughter," she said with a comforting smile. "I am no friend of Bagule. His arrogance is beginning to annoy me."

"Thank you, Nana," Amber said. She closed her eyes again. The unfamiliar shapes reappeared but now they coalesced into scenes she could understand. She saw a young chubby girl sitting with a woman she resembled, the two of them working a worn loom. The fabric they created was an elaborate pattern of blues and greens.

Amber smiled. "You miss your mother, especially the days you made kente together."

Yenge's mouth formed a circle as tears came to her eyes. She turned to her peers and their eyes widened.

Bagule stepped toward her.

"This means nothing! So, she reads Yenge's hands. Any street trickster could do the same. Does that mean she can select our new leader?"

"Then give her your hands," Grandma said. "Let us see what lies in your heart."

Amber jerked her head to Grandma, her stomach hard like stone. She did not want to be anywhere near that man. He meant to kill her. Grandma gave her an assuring nod but it did not calm her. Her stomach churned.

"I have nothing to prove," Bagule replied. "My fate, as the other candidates for Sana, lies in the hands of the wise counsel of the Elders."

"And who are you to declare such a thing?"

Jakada staggered into the room, leaning heavily on a thick staff crowned with a golden falcon. He smiled weakly at Grandma and Amber as he entered then bowed the best he could toward the Elders. Bissau rushed to him, giving the mage his shoulder to lean on.

"The true violator comes!" Bagule announced. "Here is the man who should be condemned by us all. He imprisons us with his magic yet comes and goes as he pleases. Why should we be deprived of the bounty of the outer world while he enjoys its fruits?"

"I am not the only one who has breached the barrier," Jakada replied.

"This family is polluted," Bagule said. "The Elders must choose."

Amber looked back to her great grandfather then to Bagule. Her senses roiled inside her head, obscuring her skill to read them. But she was sure of one thing; something bad was about to happen.

Jakada pointed a finger at Bagule. "You speak of my transgressions but what of yours? Did you not send Aisha to stop my daughter's return? Did you not contact bandits to do the same thing once Aisha betrayed you?"

"Enough of this!" Bagule shouted. He struck the strings of the kora hard. A sharp discordant sound filled the room. Amber's ears ached and she winched. When she opened her eyes, a brilliant bolt streaked toward her. She raised her arms to protect herself and was swallowed by light and heat as she fell to the floor. For a moment she the power consumed her, and then the sensation changed. The energy subsided and she rose on her hands and knees. She looked to her great grandfather then gasped. The light crackled from Bagule's kora to her great grandfather's extended palms. Grandma, Bissau and Aisha lay unconscious on the floor around him. She crawled toward him, the amber necklace hot against her skin.

Great grandfather looked at her.

"No Amber," he said. "You must go now!"

Amber continued to crawl to him, growing weaker with each moment. She was almost to him when someone grabbed her leg then dragged her away. She jerked her leg free then rolled onto her back to see Nieleni looming over her, a curved dagger in her hand. Nieleni lunged; Amber brought her knees to her chest then kicked out. Both feet smashed into Nieleni's face. Bagule's consort dropped the dagger as she fell onto her back. Amber struggled to her feet then jumped to her great grandfather, embracing him. She felt the necklace's power surge from her then into her great grandfather. The stream of light coalesced into a blinding sphere which burst throughout the room, knocking her to the floor. She was blinded for a moment; when her sight cleared she saw her great grandfather lying beside her. His head turned toward her and he grinned.

Amber stood. Everyone in the room was either lying on the floor or struggling to sit or stand. She studied each face before saying what she felt.

"Bagule and Nieleni are gone," she said.

Bissau and Grandma staggered to great grandfather then helped him to his feet. He looked about the room as well.

"It seems so," he said.

Amber looked into her great grandfather's eyes as heaviness set into her mind.

"Did I…did we kill them?"

Jakada patted her shoulder. "Whatever has happened to them was meant to be," he said. "Do not feel guilty."

"He is right," Grandma said as she hugged her. "Bagule had a choice. He is responsible for his fate."

Healers and servants rushed into the room moments later then set about tending the elders and others.

"We will have to postpone the selection," Jakada said.

"There is no need," Amber replied.

"What do you mean?" Bissau asked.

She gazed about the room once more.

"It is said the Sana was a great man. I did not know him. But I know something of Marai."

"Everyone! Gather about!" Bissau shouted. The elders and the others came, forming a circle around Amber, Grandma, Bissau, great grandfather and Aisha.

"Speak Amber," Jakada said.

"I must say what I feel, what is inside me," she said. "There is no one in this city worthy to take the Sana's place."

A collective gasp filled the room. Yenge stumbled back as if struck.

"What do you mean no one?" Yenge said. "There has always been a Sana!"

Amber closed her eyes, concentrating on the feelings coursing through her. She saw images of Marai from the day it was founded, faces of the men and women who had been named Sana, selected by women with her power. And as much as she tried to find someone among the people before her to continue that tradition she found none. But there was one who would be Sana one day. She did her best not to show any gesture that revealed her feelings, for that person was far from ready.

She looked at her great grandfather instead.

"When you sealed Marai from the world you did so with the best interests of both sides. It was a wise decision. But times and people change. The world can benefit from what Marai holds, and Marai can benefit from what the world holds. Bagule was right; it is time for the wall to come down. But his intentions were wrong."

"So, what do we do, Amber?" he asked.

"The Elders will rule Marai," she said. "They have always served as counsel to the Sana. Now they will issue decrees by consensus."

She took Nana Yenge's hand.

"Yours will be the final say," she said. "Your lineage is the strongest. It is your right."

"Yet I am not fit to be Sana?" Yenge questioned.

"It is what I feel," Amber answered.

The elders murmured to each other, their heads nodding in approval of Amber's words.

"You say we must let down the Veil," Yenge said. "But our people are not ready for this outside world."

Amber nodded in agreement. "Someone must teach every Maraibu the ways of the outside world, someone who has lived in both. There is no better teacher than my grandmother, Alake."

Grandma stepped forward. Great grandfather placed his hands on Grandma's shoulders. The Elders whispered among each other again then faced Amber with approving nods.

Amber relaxed. She felt as if she was being released from gentle hands. Fatigue washed over her and she staggered. A pair of familiar arms wrapped around her; she looked over her shoulder into the smiling face of Bissau.

Yenge gazed over the chamber.

"The ancestors have spoken through Jakada's daughter,' she announced. "Her words carry their wisdom. The elders will administer

Marai until that time a new Sana is ready, whenever that may be. The Veil will come down."

There was neither cheer of approval nor a roar of protest, just a consensus of head nods and grunts of assent.

Grandma and great grandfather stood before Amber. The confidence she displayed earlier trickled away.

"Thank you, Amber," great grandfather said. "You've come a long way to help us. You saved our city."

"I'm sorry I didn't pick you as Sana," she said.

Great grandfather smiled. "The truth plays no favorites. You did well."

Her eyes went to Grandma.

"You're not going back, are you?"

Grandma smiled. "No, Amber. I'm staying here."

"I didn't mean you had to stay here all the time."

Grandma stepped back her arms wide. "Look at me, Amber. Would you go back?"

Amber grinned, and then hugged Grandma tight.

"I guess not."

"It is time for you to return," great grandfather said. "Your parents must be worried."

"That's an understatement," she said. "I haven't spoken to them since we left Senegal."

"Then we must hurry," Grandma said.

"We must go to the mirror," great grandfatherreplied.

Amber's stomach tightened as she turned to face Bissau. The young man smiled as she took his hands.

"Thank you, Bissau."

"I would never let harm come to you," he said. "You are of Jakada's blood. You are like a sister to me."

Amber's smile faded. She had no intentions of being Bissau's sister.

She hugged him tight then kissed him. When she stepped back Bissau's face was frozen somewhere between shock and fear. Amber laughed.

"I'm ready to go home now," she said.

CHAPTER THIRTY-THREE

Miss Josephine lounged at her patio table, sipping on her afternoon tea when she heard voices drifting from her house. Fear gripped her and her hand went to the talisman necklace circling her elegant neckline.

"Not again!" she gasped.

She jumped from her chair, knocking over the table as the door opened. Her terror dissipated as Amber, Bissau, and a much younger Alake stepped out onto the patio.

"*Mes amis!*" she exclaimed. "*Mes beaux amis!*"

She hugged Amber tight, and then greeted her grandmother with a sisterly embrace. For Bissau she kissed his cheeks like a long-lost son.

"So, you found what you sought?" Miss Josephine asked.

The three looked at each other with warm smiles.

"Yes, we did," Amber answered. "Mademoiselle, did I leave my phone here?"

"You did, Cheri, and it's been singing ever since. I believe the artist name is Neo?"

Amber giggled. "Yes it is." She was beginning to feel like a thirteen-year-old again.

"I suspect it is your parents." Miss Josephine's face reflected their worry.

"You should call them," Grandma said.

Neo's smooth voice interrupted their conversation.

Miss Josephine rushed into her bedroom then returned with the phone. Amber took a deep breath then answered in the most innocent voice she could muster.

"Hi mommy!"

"Oh, sweet Jesus! It's my baby girl! Are you alright? Where's mama? Is she okay?" We've been..."

Her father's voice intruded.

"Young lady, you have a lot, I mean A LOT of explaining to do. Let me speak to your grandmother!"

"Daddy, everything is fine," Amber replied. "Me and Grandma are fine. We took a trip up the Niger River where our cell phones didn't work."

"What do you mean your cell phones didn't work? Cellphones work everywhere! Do you realize how worried we were? No, how worried we are? Let me speak to your grandmother!"

Amber closed her eyes then shook her head.

"Daddy, Grandma and I are in Dakar. We're catching the next plane out to Paris then home. See you soon! I love you both."

Amber hung up then muted the ringtone.

"You sure you're not coming back, Grandma?"

Grandma spread her arms then twirled around. "How would I explain this? Crystal and Joseph aren't ready. Let's get you home and settled before we spring anything else on them."

"You're right, Grandma. You're always right."

She turned to Miss Josephine. "Miss Josephine, can you suffer our company for one night? It will take time to make a flight reservation to Paris."

"Of course!" she exclaimed. "I'd be delighted!"

Miss Josephine quickly organized a dinner that resembled a feast for a diplomat. As their host and Grandma discussed her amazing physical transformation, Amber and Bissau ate silently. Amber looked at her protector as he studied his food before each bite. Occasionally he would look up then smile at her before immersing himself in his meal. She held back a laugh; she was making him nervous. After the meal Grandma and Miss Josephine retired to the parlor. Amber decided to go upstairs to the balcony. She grinned when she realized Bissau was following her.

He stood beside her as she looked out onto the ocean.

"You don't have to protect me anymore," she said.

"I know," Bissau replied.

"Thank you," she said.

"There is no need to thank me. Baba Jakada gave me a duty."

"But you didn't have to do it."

Bissau's eyes widened. "Of course, I did. Baba Jakada is my master. I do as he commands."

Amber turned. "You mean you are his slave?"

Bissau shook his head. "He is my…mentor. In order to learn I must do everything he asks. It is our way."

"We are so different," she said.

"No, we're not," Bissau replied. "In the heart we are all the same. You should know this."

She did. It was why standing so close to Bissau made her nervous. She knew how she felt about him and she knew he felt the same.

"Bissau, I…"

"I don't think we should speak on such things," he said. "Although Master Jakada treats me like an equal, I am not. There is no way we can marry."

"Marry? Nobody said anything about marrying! I'm only thirteen, and even if I was older marrying would be the last thing on my mind."

Bissau's face sagged, his eyes drooping. Amber reached for him and he pulled away.

"I didn't mean it like that," she corrected. "Things are different outside Marai. In this world people our age aren't considered adults. We aren't allowed to get married. Not that I'm saying I would marry you if we were allowed…wait a minute, I didn't mean that either."

"I know what you meant," Bissau said.

"No, I don't think you do."

Amber suddenly felt very tired. Moments ago, she was deciding the fate of a city, and now she couldn't find the right words to say to a boy.

"I'm going to sleep," she finally said.

She left Bissau on the balcony and retired to her room. The entire experience seemed to gang up on her at that moment, hitting her with exhaustion and a sense of relief. She had a dreamless sleep, awaking to a bright morning. Grandma peered at her from the doorway, a proud smile on her face.

"Wake up, baby girl. It's time."

The exhaustion from the day before yielded to the excitement of going home. Though she cherished every aspect of her adventure, Amber was homesick. She sat at the table with Grandma, Miss Josephine and Bissau, who still carried that sour look from the day before. Amber paid him no mind. She was going home. In a few days, Bissau would be a memory, a pleasant, cute memory.

"You must be very excited!" Miss Josephine sang.

"I am!" Amber replied.

"So, what is the first thing you'll do?"

"Hug my Mama and Daddy then get me a hamburger!"

Grandma and Miss Josephine laughed; Bissau looked up from his plate with solemn eyes but said nothing.

After breakfast Amber packed her things. She called Mama and Daddy; assuring them she was actually coming home and avoiding any questions about why Grandma wasn't. The four of them climbed into Miss Josephine's limousine then rode to the airport, Amber clinging to Grandma's arm the entire ride. Occasionally she peered out the window, taking a long look at Dakar. She knew this wouldn't be the last time she visited, but she hoped she'd be away long enough to miss it. Returning to Marai would mean serious things were afoot, and she'd had her fill of serious for a while.

They arrived at the airport an hour before her flight. Miss Josephine was well respected in Dakar, so the check-in process went quickly. Airport security allowed them to accompany her to her gate.

"Goodbye, cheri," Miss Josephine said as she hugged her. "You be a good girl, and make sure you tell your parents that Miss Josephine took good care of you."

"I will," Amber said.

She hugged Grandma long and tight.

"I love you so much, Grandma," she whispered as tears welled in her eyes. "Thank you for this."

"I'm the one who should be thanking you, baby girl."

Grandma stepped back, holding her at arm's length.

"You've grown so much this summer. I'm glad to be a part of it. Now don't you worry about your Mama and Daddy. I'll have a long conversation with them while you're on your way home. By the time you land in Atlanta everything will be fine."

Amber smirked. "No, it won't."

Grandma chuckled. "No, it probably won't, but it will be better than when you leave here."

Bissau appeared beside Grandma with her bag. His expression was cool.

"Are you ready?" he asked. "The plane is boarding."

Amber emotions dampened. He was in so much turmoil inside.

"Maybe I should have used a mirror," she joked.

Bissau's expression didn't change and Amber's smile faded.

"Yes, I'm ready," she said.

He placed the bag at her feet.

"Goodbye, Amber. Be safe."

Bissau sulked away. Grandma watched him with concern.

"What did you say to him?" she asked.

"The wrong things," Amber answered. "But it's for the best. We're so different."

Grandma smiled. "Get on the plane, baby. Call me when you get settled."

"I will, grandma."

Amber hugged Grandma one more time. She peered over Grandma's shoulder and waved at Bissau. He looked at her then shared a weak smile. Amber kept smiling at him as she boarded the plane despite the sadness inside her. It was for the best, she thought. It had to be.

It was a solemn flight to Paris. She should have been happier returning home, but she was missing Grandma already. She missed Bissau, too. Why couldn't there be a boy like him waiting for her in Atlanta, a boy that respected her and thought the world of her?

The flight was late to Paris so she had just enough time to grab a bite to eat then board the non-stop to Atlanta. She slept the entire flight, fatigue finally catch up to her.

"Honey, we're landing."

The flight attendant's voice startled her. She opened her eyes to a pleasant female face.

"We're landing, sugar. You need to raise your seat."

Amber scrambled about for the lever then lifted her backrest.

The flight attendant smiled. "There you go. Love your head wrap."

Amber beamed. "Thank you!"

She looked out the window. The homesickness flared as they cruised by Stone Mountain, the huge solitary piece of granite a definitive sign that she was home. The familiar cluster of high-rises before her sealed the deal. She thought she would be more nervous but she wasn't; despite Grandma's calls she would still have a lot of explaining to do. But that was okay. She was home, and that was all that mattered.

It felt like forever for the plane to touch the tarmac then cruise to the gate. Amber, usually patient when exiting, jumped out of her seat as soon as the seatbelt light turned off. She grabbed her bag from the overhead bin then joined the shuffling line to the cabin door. As soon as she had room she fast walked through the terminal to the escalator leading to the trains. No sooner did she enter the train did she call her mother.

"Mama?"

"We're here baby," Mama answered.

"I'll be there in a minute," Amber replied.

She was one of the first off the train and on the escalator. Amber jogged up the moving stairs. As she emerged from the corridor she saw her mother holding a big sign embellished with her name.

"Welcome home, Amber!" they shouted.

She didn't know whether to be embarrassed or happy, so he decided to be embarrassedly happy.

Amber and her mother squealed together as they ran to each other and hugged.

"Hey baby!" Mama said.

"Hey mommy!" Amber replied.

She looked over Mama's shoulder. Daddy sauntered to them, a big smile on his face. He'd grown a beard during vacation as he usually did. It looked good on him. He wrapped his thick arms around both of them.

"Now this is how our vacation should have been," he said. "Welcome home, princess."

Daddy's words sent her back to Marai. There she was a princess, sort of.

"Hey, Daddy. It's good to be home."

They walked to the shuttle then rode to the car in silence. Mama hugged her the entire way as Daddy whistled one of his favorite tunes. For the first time in her life she looked at her parents with her inner eye, enhanced by her journey to Marai. She found what she expected; good, loving people who only wanted the best for her. She would make the best of private school, she decided. If the journey to Marai taught her anything it was the difference between inconvenience and crisis. She snuggled against Mama then closed her eyes, falling into a peaceful sleep.

CHAPTER THIRTY-FOUR

Amber straightened her tie one last time then stepped back from her mirror for a final inspection. She frowned; there was no way to make the uniform look good. Otherwise she was ready for her first day at Clifton Academy. The summer had been more than she could ever imagine. She gazed into the mirror and a smile came to her face.

"I wonder if Grandma can see me?" she whispered. Her eyes widened as another thought came to her head.

"I wonder if Bissau can see me?" Her smile grew wider despite the touch of melancholy in her heart. She would see him again, but he would probably be a married man. They were different people living in different worlds. She wished she could control her heart as much as she could read others. Then she wouldn't waste her time crushing on men and boys she had no chance of dating.

"Are we ready?"

Mama burst into the room, her face glowing.

"Ooh, my girl looks marvelous!"

Amber frowned. "You can't look marvelous in a school uniform, mama. You look acceptable. That's what school uniforms are for."

"I'm not trying to hear your brooding today," Mama replied. "My baby looks good in that uniform. You're working it like a runway model. Clifton Academy better watch out!"

Amber grinned despite herself.

"Let me see!"

Daddy entered her room dressed for work.

"That uniform looks like a gown on you," he said.

"Y'all need to stop," Amber laughed. "Isn't it time to go?"

Mama looked at her watch. "Yes it is! Come on Robinson family!"

Amber grabbed her backpack then followed Mama and Daddy out of the room.

"Oh, wait a minute!"

She trotted back to her desk, grabbing her amber necklace. It clashed with her uniform but that didn't matter.

Daddy and Mama kissed before Daddy climbed into his Audi sedan then drove off to work. It was a first day for him as well, the first day as vice president of Sankofa Communications. Amber climbed in the Honda with Mama then fastened her seatbelt.

"Can we drive by the bus stop?" she asked.

Mama gave her a sympathetic smile. "Yes, we can."

Mama took the brief detour that passed the bus stop. Jasmine was there, dressed impeccably for her first day of public high school. Amber rolled down the window.

"Hey queen!" she shouted.

"Hey queen!" Jasmine shouted back. A few other friends shouted as well. A pang hit Amber as she rolled up her window.

Mama patted her shoulder. "It's going to be okay, baby. You'll see your old friends on the weekend and you'll make new friends at Clifton. If it's one thing Robinsons are good at is making friends. Besides, this is an outstanding opportunity for you."

"I know mama," Amber replied. It all made sense but it didn't change how she felt. No matter how great Clifton Academy turned out to be, high school would be ten times better with her old friends at Julian High.

Amber stared out the window the entire ride to Clifton Academy. Mama turned onto the magnolia tree lined brick paved entrance leading to the school. A parade of luxury cars moved through the roundabout, Mama's Honda standing out among them. She didn't like that at all.

"I can't wait till I get my Lexus!"

Amber grinned then patted mama on the shoulder. "It will be okay, baby."

Mama laughed. "Get out my car!"

They kissed; Amber grabbed her backpack then entered her new world.

She followed the crowd through the archway and into the main building. She'd visited the school for orientation so she knew her way around. Homeroom was down the main hallway past the freshman lockers to the left, three doors down on the right. She entered the class room of Elizabeth Perry, her homeroom teacher. The middle-aged woman reminded Amber of Grandma, which was comforting. A cute salt and pepper afro crowned her head, her face graced with a pair of small round glasses. She wore a dress that was definitely Afrocentric but not from Senegal. Miss Perry greeted everyone with an inviting smile. Her eyes lingered on Amber and she found herself scrutinizing the teacher with her skills. She was a good person, but there was something inside. Amber would let her keep her secret.

"Welcome to Clifton Academy!" Miss Perry announced. "I'm Elizabeth Perry, your guide for your inaugural year at our outstanding institution. I'm sure you're all aware of our illustrious history, so I won't bore you with the details."

Amber laughed with her classmates as she scanned their faces. If she was at Julian she would recognize most of them. Here, she was a stranger among friends.

Miss Perry continued her speech. "At Clifton you'll be challenged to the limit of your abilities. Your curiosity will be sparked and your intelligence tested. If you make it to your senior year you will be the best person you could possibly be. This is not a promise. It is a guarantee."

The classroom door opened, interrupting Miss Perry's speech.

"Can I help you?" she asked.

Amber looked with the rest of the class then caught her breath. Standing at the door looking awkward in his school uniform was Bissau. The smile that came to her face was as joyful as she felt.

"I am sorry to disturb you," he said in heavily accented English. "The principal told me report to this room."

"Please, come in," Miss Perry said. Bissau sauntered in, glancing at Amber as he made his way to the homeroom teacher. He handed her his information.

"Bissau Keita," she said aloud. "You're Bambara?"

"Soninke," he replied. "I'm from Ma...Senegal."

"Welcome to my class, Bissau. Please take a seat."

Bissau took an empty seat near the rear of the class. The remainder of Miss Perry's speech was garbled talk to Amber. She kept peeking back at Bissau and smiling. The bell for first period didn't sound fast enough.

"What are you doing here?" she said as she hurried to his desk. She hugged him before he could answer.

"I've been sent to teach you," he answered.

Amber pulled away. "Teach me? What?"

Bissau nodded. "You have shown that your abilities are far beyond that of a Seer. Jele Jakada has instructed me to help you develop them."

"How are you going to teach me?" she asked. "You're just an acolyte...I mean, you're still learning, too."

"That's true, but I have more training than you. I will show you what I know. The rest of your training will have to take place in Marai."

"So, I'll have to go back," Amber said.

"Yes," Bissau answered.

"What about Bagule?" Amber asked.

Bissau's eyes narrowed. "Bagule is gone but there may be others. You must be ready."

Amber's stomach tightened. She remembered how Bagule tried to hurt her and how she responded. This was her responsibility, but she still doubted her ability to do what was asked of her. It seemed that life wasn't supposed to be simple for her.

"What's your first class?" she asked, eager to change the subject.

"Algebra," he replied.

"Good! Mine, too. Let's walk together."

Amber locked her arm with his and they left the room.

"I'm glad you're here Bissau," she said.

"I'm glad I'm here too, Amber."

They shared a smile then walked arm in arm through the halls of Clifton Academy. Amber stole another glance at Bissau. Private school might not be so bad after all.

ABOUT THE AUTHOR

Milton Davis is owner of MVmedia, LLC, a micro publishing company specializing in Science Fiction, Fantasy and Sword and Soul. MVmedia's mission is to provide speculative fiction books that represent people of color in a positive manner. Milton is the author of ten novels; his most recent is the Steamfunk adventure From Here to Timbuktu. He is the editor and co-editor of seven anthologies; The City, Dark Universe with Gene Peterson; Griots: A Sword and Soul Anthology and Griot: Sisters of the Spear, with Charles R. Saunders; The Ki Khanga Anthology, the Steamfunk! Anthology, and the Dieselfunk anthology with Balogun Ojetade. MVmedia has also published Once Upon A Time in Afrika by Balogun Ojetade and Abegoni: First Calling by Sword and Soul creator and icon Charles R. Saunders. Milton is also a co-writer of the award-winning script, Ngolo and recently as the Hal Clement Science Speaker for Boskone 54.

Milton resides in Metro Atlanta with his wife Vickie and his children Brandon and Alana.

9 780980 084276